BLUE THREADS AND OTHER STORIES

MATTHEW KUNASHE CHIKONO

Mwanaka Media and Publishing Pvt Ltd,
Chitungwiza, Zimbabwe

*

Creativity, Wisdom, and Beauty

Publisher: *Mmap*

Mwanaka Media and Publishing Pvt Ltd

24 Svosve Road, Zengeza 1

Chitungwiza, Zimbabwe

mwanaka@yahoo.com

mwanaka13@gmail.com

https://www.mmapublishing.org

www.africanbookscollective.com/publishers/mwanaka-media-and-publishing

https://facebook.com/MwanakaMediaAndPublishing/

Distributed in and outside N. America by African Books Collective

orders@africanbookscollective.com

www.africanbookscollective.com

ISBN: 978-1-77933-144-1

EAN: 9781779331441

DISCLAIMER

All views expressed in this publication are those of the author and do not necessarily reflect the views of *Mmap*.

TABLE OF CONTENTS

Introduction

Blue Threads and Other Stories is my second solo short story collection. This collection took a great deal out of me during its crafting. I wrote most of the stories when events of my own life were in every sense appearing to be a work of fiction. There's a great sense of my struggles within these stories, I suppose I aimed to write something that would stare back at me and truly identify the path I had taken.

Stories such as *Blue Threads, Coming Home, Home for Christmas, A Special Place, Mourning* and *Sunset* portray a rather gloomy picture of the world that surrounded me hence also the state of my mind at the time. Ironically it was the happiest period of my life to this day. I cannot say I consciously put together every single element of the stories, most of the details were a consequence of the flow of the stories and were perhaps the dread of my mind.

While I was personally happy at that moment, having been going through the cycles of life, there was always that feeling that the pendulum would oscillate the other way. Perhaps that explains why these stories unfolded the way they did!

Stories with speculative elements of science fiction and fantasy such as *For Her Only, A Little Song for the Young One* and *The Little Switch*, tear down fabrics of reality. Hope, happiness, love and birth, all the joys in this world, also have a tone of sadness to them reminding everyone that even the worlds we create are not always perfect.

In the end, I found myself extremely satisfied with the work and felt rather strongly that all the stories would come together and form a complete collection that spans through time and the multiverse.

Dedication

In memory of Emma Moyo who departed this realm on 02/11/13

For Her Only

The boy didn't look his age, he was seven summers old but looked much younger than that. His frail body, from head to toe, was covered with goat and cow skins. They, the animal skins, were warm enough against the winter wind that had been raging for some days. The cold had frozen every bit of happiness in the village. The boy, plump and warm, had left the rest of the cold and hunger-stricken-children glued to their mothers' breasts, mothers who were trying to warm their own bodies with single pieces of charcoal. That day, like every other day, the boy had come to talk to the fish. The fish were always happy and ready to give joy to their visitor.

The boy staggered upstream, skipping upon the rocks making sure not to get his feet wet. He could see his village a distance away, downstream. Thirty or so huts clustered around the Chief's kraal, all of which were surrounded by a wall of stone and mortar. That was the only home the boy had ever known.

Of course, he wasn't allowed to wander off that far from the village, but he knew no one would notice. Not his mother; she was the only healer in the village, always administering herbs to the old and the sick for the entire day. Not his father, the Chief, he was rich and always fixing the villagers' lives. They did not care about the boy, but the fishes did. The fishes would console and give the boy the love he deserved. With this in mind the boy's resolve to reach the pond where the fishes waited for him was strengthened. He could see the pond a few paces away.

Then, the pond exploded right in front of his eyes.

A large body of water rose some feet into the air before splashing back to the pond. The boy stood still. His happy fishes were thrown out of the water. Some of the fishes were stuck in the trees. The boy could not fathom what had happened. He watched the pond suspiciously from a little distance away.

As the murky water settled, the boy could see a large fish, twice as large as he was, inside the water. Surely this was magic. Then it popped its head from the water and started coughing and gasping for air. The fish had a human head, a woman's head. A chill ran through the boy's spine. He had heard tales of children abducted by mermaids only to be returned to their families decades later. The boy didn't want to live in a cave under the water, eating worms the mermaid would offer him.

The boy took one step back. The mermaid swam to the edge of the pond. The boy couldn't run away, not yet anyways, he had to see the mermaid's hind which was said to be that of a fish. The mermaid dragged itself out of the pond and crawled to the higher ground with its own two feet.

The boy screamed. The only mermaid he had ever seen happened to have a woman's head and torso but a pair of legs. It was scary and deserved a scream from the boy. Hearing the boy scream, the mermaid turned to the direction of the boy and screamed even louder. It grabbed a stone and threw it in the boy's direction. The stone missed by far and fell in the middle of the pond.

"No!" The mermaid jumped into the pond, and started searching furiously where the stone had sunk, "look what you have made me do."

The boy didn't know what he had done. He wasn't sure if he was supposed to apologise. He took that moment to observe the mermaid standing waist deep in the water. It was young and pretty enough to conform to the legendary beauty of the mermaids. It could have been a mermaid, but her hair was short, black, and rugged. Her face was pale, not the usual dark complexion the boy was accustomed to seeing in his village. The boy thought she was beautiful and wanted to marry her. Impala skins, which was what she wore, were rare and reserved only for the noble village elders. The usual necklaces, beads and wristbands didn't interest the boy.

The mermaid walked out of the pond, turning back after every step, hoping to find the stone she had thrown earlier. Between the glances the boy noticed the woman's belly poking out of her animal skins, she was pregnant.

"Where are the rest of the villagers?" the mermaid asked the boy, who only pointed downstream with his shaky finger. The mermaid looked closely at the boy for the first time. It didn't know what to make of him, "What is your name boy?"

"Khumalo." The boy stammered back. The mermaid's face saddened at the name. It looked past the boy, all the way to its own past.

"Khumalo. I once knew someone named Khumalo." It recalled with sorrow.

The mermaid took one last glance at the pond and eagerly made its way down to the village, caressing its huge stomach.

***

Years of experience had taught Rati that it was easy to slice open a bream in one hand motion. That way she would spare herself from the fins that could easily stick her fingers together. She hummed the song her mother had always sang to her. Singing always made chores seem easy. In no time she had sliced open four breams and cleaned out the intestines and was ready to leave to barter with the villagers.

"Singing your witch song again?"

The voice startled Rati but she quickly regained her composure after she noticed it was Khumalo who had sneaked behind her again. She gave him a sly smile and continued with her fish.

"I told you not to startle me when I am doing chores, my mother doesn't like it." Rati said, pointing to her mother who was standing in the river staring intently at the waters.

Rati had lived on the riverbank with her mother for as long as she remembered. It had always been the two of them, well, three of them, counting Khumalo who had visited every single day. Since she was a baby, Khumalo had come all the way from the village to play with her, none of the children wanted to play with her. She and her mother had never been welcome to stay in the village. Her mother had built a shack from mud and branches and had raised her daughter in it by fishing in the river every day. She was the only fisherwoman known in all the lands.

"I will tell you again, it's not a witch song. It's a hymn a trope-bearer uses to prepare the way. I told you what a trope is right?"

"You already told me, Rati," Khumalo said with resignation," it is the magical boulder that carried your mother to this land."

Rati sighed. Despite her mother's warning Rati had told Khumalo about the trope, a magical rock that needed incantations to open channels to travel to distant lands. Rati's mother had travelled from those distant lands years ago. She had lost the rock on the first day she had arrived. If her mother was not mistaken the rock lay somewhere in the river. For sixteen years her mother had woken up every morning in search of the rock in the chilly water.

Her mother had told her it was a secret between mother and daughter; but Rati was of age now and would need a husband soon. Khumalo, being a Chief's son and a close family friend, was a prospect she didn't want to miss so why keep a secret from someone who would marry her?

"Khumalo, can you accompany me to the village? Rati asked. "I have to trade this basket of fish with the blacksmith"

She knew he would say yes. She had planned it all to happen that way. In preparation for her walk in the village with Khumalo, she had waxed the goat skins she wore. She had to make sure every other girl in the village knew that Rati was laying claim to the Chief's son.

Khumalo, unable to say no to the prettiest face he knew, grabbed Rati's basket and led the way, awkwardly glancing at her as she followed in his heels, a smile of triumph on her face.

*

It was just a pond, but they had already started calling her the lady of the lake, a mockery to what she did every day. Except when she was sleeping, she was always in the water looking for the trope. The fish just came to her but what she needed was the trope. She had been searching for it for sixteen years, every single day of them.

On that day she was standing in the water, searching for her way out. She stood up to stretch her back and noticed her daughter cleaning the breams she had caught earlier that morning. Her daughter was as beautiful as a mermaid, none of the girls in the village could compare to her.

On the night of her daughter's birth, the lady of the lake had seen the beauty of what she had given to the world. A girl with no father,

10

a creature who would suffer the wrath of the world. She gave the little child her own name, Rati. The lady of the lake was sure that her own daughter would suffer the way she had suffered. She was not happy about it, but it was the curse of being raised by a single mother.

Rati, the mother, noticed her daughter cleaning the fish, oblivious to the Chief's son sneaking up behind her. The daughter was startled for a moment but relaxed a bit when she saw who it was. Then the two started to talk. She was too far to hear anything but from the way her daughter blushed, she knew everything there was.

"It's a good thing that she fell in love with the Chief's son. If she gets to marry him, she will live comfortably for the rest of her life," She said under her breath.

As if on cue the two love birds started to walk towards the village. The boy carrying the basket with the fish whilst the girl followed behind him with a grin on her face. The boy looked happy. Khumalo - that was the boy's name. The Lady of the lake felt ashamed of herself for not remembering the boy's name.

On her first day on this strange land she had met Khumalo, a seven-year-old boy then. He had startled her, and she had lost the trope, she didn't blame him though. The boy had led her to the village. The villagers did not accept her into their home, she was pregnant but without a husband. They, however, allowed her to build her own shelter near the river. The boy has been fascinated by her belly. He had visited almost every day in her pregnancy months. Upon the arrival of Rati, the daughter, the boy had started visiting every day to play with the child. Sixteen years later they were about to get married. Rati the mother wasn't disappointed. All she wanted was her daughter not tell Khumalo about the trope.

As Rati and Khumalo disappeared towards the village, Rati the mother then decided to take a break from her search. It was way past midday after all, and she had other duties to attend to.

Everything would had been easier if he were there.

She hadn't thought about him in years, Sifelani, the father of her daughter. The last time she saw Sifelani, he lay in a pool of his own blood slowly dying from a stab wound. Rati the mother had only glanced once and continued singing the song of the trope bearer. The trope had opened the channels, she had escaped with her yet-to-be-born child. That was the day she had lost her husband and her peace.

As Rati the mother came out of her reverie, she heaved herself out of the water. Just then, she slipped and hit her face on a turtle's back. She broke a tooth. She glared at the turtle; she hadn't seen one in ages. She picked it up and closely examined it. The turtle was heavier than expected. It was just a rock. A hiss of disappointment escaped her mouth. She threw the stone near the fireplace, intending to make it a base stone for her cooking pots.

She didn't notice the fire she had lighted thereafter melt the dirt around the new stone neither did she notice the familiar design of the trope appearing on the stone. She didn't notice the trope she had hauled in the pond years earlier glowing beside the fire.

*

Khumalo walked slowly, his bare feet crushing dead autumn leaves on the ground. Years had passed since he had visited Rati in his impala hide. He now wore a cheetah hide; he wasn't a nobody anymore in village. In his hand he held a long spear. The spear that the royal and the elite only held.

The well-trodden path was familiar to his feet, he could walk all the way with his eyes closed. It was almost evening as he made his way to the lone hut. A flock of birds flew away as he came closer to the hut. No smoke came from the vents or the entrance, Khumalo thought the house was empty.

For a while he thought of going home and coming back the following day, but he decided against it. Whatever was on his mind he had to talk to Rati that day. He was ready to profess his love to her.

He sat outside the hut and waited for her. Between the croaking frogs, the chirping crickets, and a distant laughter of hyenas, Khumalo heard a song. Someone was singing inside Rati's hut. Without thinking much Khumalo budged into the hut.

From the dimming fire Khumalo could see a woman kneeling in front of a glowing stone. Strange sounds were coming out of her mouth. It took a moment to realise it was Rati's mother. Sensing the presence of another person the woman turned around to see him glaring at her. She screamed and stood stork still, shocked.

"Khumalo!" She ejaculated, "You scared me."

Khumalo kept his eyes on the glowing stone. He noticed it changing colour to black. It definitely was the trope.

"I didn't know you were coming. I was going to speak to you at your ascension tonight. Congratulations Chief Khumalo!"

"Sifelani, Chief Sifelani. That is the name I am taking upon my ascension to the chieftain tonight." Khumalo spoke softly, surprised at his own ability to keep his composure.

"Rati is not here my son, I will tell her you stopped by." The mother said picking up the trope and neatly wrapping it in cowhides. She could see Khumalo eyeing it.

13

"That's the trope, isn't it?" The boy started," You don't have to lie, Rati had told me all about it. You want to travel to other worlds, taking Rati with you, and leaving me all alone?"

Rati's mother was taken aback by the gentle boy's sudden outburst. She mumbled something about the trope not working well and leaving Rati behind. Before she could think of a good reply the boy struck her on the forehead with a log from the fire. She didn't even scream; she just fell dead on the floor. Without giving it much thought, Khumalo grabbed the trope and dug a small hole on the fireplace. He hid the trope inside the hole and covered it with some ash. No one would ever think of looking there.

The realization that he had murdered a woman in her own hut suddenly dawned upon him. Not sure what to do next, the boy who was soon-to-be chief continued staring at the woman on the floor. The dim hut exponentiating the gloominess of the situation. He wasn't sure what was happening, he stood there looking sheepishly until he heard a voice singing and footsteps approaching the hut.

"Mother?"

*

Chief Sifelani led the procession, few strides behind him his wife followed, then came the rest of the villagers. The villagers had been told that on arriving at the riverbank they had to stop whilst the Chief and his wife continued to make their way to the old hut.

"Chief Sifelani," the woman called, "can we take a moment to rest?"

"I am sorry my love I keep forgetting your condition." the Chief said, helping the woman to sit on the ground.

14

The woman giggled. She knew her husband loved her but hated it when she called him Chief Sifelani, he was always Khumalo to her. The husband caressed her stomach. She was heavily pregnant with their first child.

"We should continue walking," the woman continued, "I haven't seen my mother's place in a long time."

It was almost a year since Rati had left her home. The night she left; she had come back home from fetching firewood from the forest to find the Chief standing upon her mother's body. Rati had almost lost her sanity then, begging her dead mother to come back to life.

The Chief had calmed her. He had told Rati how he had come to visit them and discovered Rati's mother laying on the floor with blood coming out of her cracked skull. In between the sobs and the mourning, Rati had asked about the trope her mother had found. The Chief didn't know anything, and they had searched everywhere together but to no avail.

"I will postpone my ascension tonight," the boy had proclaimed, "I will find whoever did this to your mother and punish them. Tonight, come with me to the village, I will marry you and take care of you for the rest of your life."

Rati had left to become Chief Sifelani's wife. They had laid her mother to rest the following day. Chief Sifelani had searched for the murderer for several months but didn't find him. A year later the husband and the wife were going to Rati's mother's hut for her final memorial rites. The dilapidated hut was still as gloomy as ever.

Rati walked inside the hut, repeating her mother's name over and over again, praying to the ancestors to accept her mother's spirit. She did not know any of her mother's ancestors, so her prayers were short. The Chief stood at the entrance with a resigned look on his face, his mind wandering to distant lands he didn't know much about.

"When I was born," Rati said when she was done with the prayers," my mother buried my umbilical cord on the centre of the fireplace. That way I was tethered to this place and I will always come back home whatever happens."

Like a manic, the woman started to dig the fireplace with her fingers. The husband was slow to stop her. Instead of finding her umbilical cord her fingers hit the hard-cold trope.

"Khumalo," Rati started, "this is my mother's Trope."

Chief Sifelani nodded slowly, not sure how it would end this time. He formulated a half-baked lie, but it died on his lips with some confusion.

"Do you know what it means?" She asked with awe on her face.

Yes, he knew what it meant. The world had been opened to her, and she would leave him. Even if he followed her, he wouldn't be a chief but a nobody. If he stayed, she would take their child and leave him. She would leave him, she the only love he had known. He didn't want to live without her, he knew he couldn't live without her.

"I can't let you do that," Chief Sifelani said to the wife who had already started chanting the song of the trope-bearer," Rati, I can't let you go to those distant lands."

Rati's face fell, perplexed by her husband's adamant answer. She stopped chanting in order to explain to her husband that what they had found was worth more than anything in the world. She turned in the direction of her husband to find him walking towards her with a blade in hand.

She froze. This was something she hadn't expected. She threw the trope in Chief Sifelani's direction with all her mighty. The trope hit home, and a moan of pain escaped his mouth. The blade fell first, then the man followed. She grabbed the blade and stabbed the man she loved. He screamed then groaned in pain. She didn't stop stabbing.

The screams alerted the people they had left at the bank and Rati heard the sound of their feet as they ran towards the hut. She looked at her husband lying in a pool of his own blood. She sat on the floor and started chanting the song of the trope bearer. She could feel the trope getting warm, she could see it start glowing.

The footsteps reached the hut entrance. The trope was glowing but not working. Rati knew that her punishment for killing the Chief would be death. She couldn't let them take her alive, it was better if she died by her own hand. She stood up, the trope in hand, dashed out of the hut and ran past the confused multitude. She jumped into the river; drowning was a better way to die.

Rati could feel herself swallowing lots of water. She went deeper into the water. No, drowning wasn't a good option. Rati changed her mind and decided to get out of the water. Rati pushed her head out of the water and swam to the edge of the river. She crawled to a higher ground where the water couldn't reach her. A scream pierced her ear. Startled, she turned and screamed back even louder. Thinking that it was one of the villagers trying to capture her. Rati hurled the thing nearest to her, realising a little late that it was the trope she had thrown. A little splash told her it had fallen somewhere in the water.

"No!" Rati screamed at the boy who seemed to be the one who screamed first. She quickly started searching the side she had heard the splash, "Look what you have made me do."

The boy looked to be six or seven and Rati had never seen him before. She started walking towards the boy who looked nervous standing on the riverbank. The rest of the villagers were not in sight.

"Where are the rest of the villagers?" she asked the boy, who pointed down the river," what is your name, boy?"

"Khumalo." The boy stammered a reply.

"Khumalo. I once knew someone named Khumalo." Rati said with a death-pale face, she recalled Khumalo the boy she had loved, the boy she had made a husband, and the husband she had killed.

This story first appeared on omenana.com issue 21 April 2022

Twenty-four

You're sitting on a dirty street bench. You don't mind the dust tainting your white dress, neither are you worried that you might breathe the dust. Your head and face are covered in hijab, you are safe from the pollutants and the eyes of passers-by who might recognise you. You don't want anyone knowing that you are in the city of Abuja. How would anyone understand that what you are doing isn't wrong?

Then you see her. She is coming from a private clinic she works in, her clean white nurse's uniform brightening the smelly and noisy city. She looks both ways before crossing the one-way street, for a second you can see her face. Goddamn, she is beautiful. She is young too, maybe in her early twenties. Her lumpy short frame is attractive to your eyes. You start to understand why your husband is having an affair with her.

She crosses the road and starts walking towards you. Instantly you start feeling sweat trickling down in your clothing. She walks slowly and confidently, sure of every step she takes. You look up to her face, ready to confront her if she recognises what you are. She passes by without even a glance. You almost cry with relief. You weren't sure you would survive a confrontation with her.

She continues to walk down the road until she reaches a parking lot. She fumbles in her handbag for a second before she unlocks a Honda Civic. It's possible that your husband bought it for her whilst you, his wife of twenty-four years, doesn't even have a driver's license. You brush the thought aside. You don't know how much nurses earn, it's probably that she bought it herself. You chuckle at the thought.

There is no way that girl would buy anything for herself, with such a pretty face somebody in Abuja is willing to buy her a yacht!

Rage blazes inside of you. You stand up and stride to the car. Whatever happens now you are ready to tell her that she is having an affair with your husband. You have been an obedient and dutiful wife for twenty-four years, surely Allah will guide and protect you. You knock on the car's window.

You knock again before the girl rolls down the window. She is crying. You just stand there gaping, not sure what to do with the anger inside of you. You mumble something about the direction to the bus terminus. Between the tear wiping and the nose cleansing, she doesn't hear you. She orders you to repeat the question.

"Are you okay?" You ask her, your instincts taking over, you are not sure if they are maternal or the love you learnt from the Quran.

"I am alright," she giggles as she wipes the last of the mucus on her nose," My therapist told me to give myself some time to cry. I chose 5.10 pm to 5.20 pm every day. It's normal. I am fine really."

She doesn't give you a chance to repeat your question. She goes on to give you a detailed direction of the streets and roads you have to follow to reach the terminus where you will find the bus to take you back to your village. You already knew the way; you thank her anyways and start making your way there.

You leave the girl alone in the car. She is probably half of your age. What is it that your husband of twenty-four years sees in this twenty-four-year-old? Offspring maybe? You haven't given your husband a child in your union. Will this girl give him plenty of sons? You doubt it, these young women won't sacrifice their careers to be housewives like what you did. It was a different time back then when you quit school to marry him. You didn't know him, but you knew you would love him. Did he ever learn to cherish you as his wife?

You arrive at the terminus and find your bus. It's half full, it will take another hour before all the seats are filled up and you can all make your way to the village. You call your sister to pass time.

"Did you find her?" She asks as soon as she picks up the phone.

"No, I don't think that was the correct clinic." You lie to her.

"I am sure it was the right clinic. Try again next week. If you find the whore who wants to break your marriage, break her neck first!" She whispers into your ear. She has been divorced twice, your sister, and she doesn't know anything about marriage.

"I surely will." You promise her, softly, "I am sure it's just a misunderstanding. If I ask my husband, he will clear all this up."

You know you are lying to your sister, and to yourself. You have always known about your husband and twenty-four-year-old women. The nurse isn't the first, you have stalked dozens before and never told a soul. A couple of months down the line your husband will lose interest, and you will be his only woman. Whatever happens you will not let go off him.

This story was first published in Our Stories Defined Anthology September 2022

Blue Threads

There was an old pay phone at the bus station, near where I was living with my uncle. It was a perfect place to call her, as I was enveloped in the privacy of the booth. After the third ring, she always picked up. She would always answer; she was unemployed and had no hobby.

"Hello?" Her uncertain voice would echo from the other end of the receiver, "Milton is that you?"

I would grunt or just keep quiet, neither confirming nor declining the given name. She didn't care either, she would then start talking whatever was on her mind that day.

"A strange man is trying to rob our house," one day she told me, her voice loud with excitement, "he has passed by our house on a bicycle twice this week."

My heart skipped a bit. Fortunately, she didn't hear it. She went on to tell me how this young man, black as coal, had slowly cycled as he passed on her front yard. The youth had closely looked at her house, only her house, as if searching for something and had passed along. She was hidden in the garden; he didn't notice her. That was the first day.

"Then today he passed by again," she continued with much vigour that I hadn't heard from her for a long time, "he was wearing the same black hat, brown jacket and black trousers. He saw me squatting and forking my garden. For a moment I thought he was going to disembark from the bicycle and ask for a job or something but then he changed his mind and sped off."

She had grown accustomed to my silence that she didn't give me a time to speak. She promised me she would be safe and would use the gun her husband kept in the garage if the man ever came back again.

"Milton, do you think I should tell my husband about this man?" She asked and was answered with my heavy breathing on the receiver.

"I won't tell him," her voice was filled with resignation, "he will think I am making it up just to have his attention. Or I am a weakling who always need his rescue at the first sign of trouble."

It was around five when she was done talking. She told me she had to go and prepare supper for her husband before he arrived from work. She dropped the receiver after she said her goodbye. She already knew there would be no answer from the other side of the phone.

***

In May 1982 l left Buhera for Harare. My uncle Jokonya had heard how I had passed my 'Ordinary' levels exams and had finally accepted my request to live with him in Kambuzuma whilst I looked for a job in the city centre. I had done extremely well in mathematics and uncle Jokonya had promised it was the gateway to a perfect job with a huge salary. I was still twenty-one and could believe anything I was told by any adult. An adult being anyone older than me, I wasn't one yet.

I waited the entire day at Mbare Msika bus terminal for my uncle to come and pick me up. He blamed his supervisor for coming late but the reeking stench of alcohol on him screamed of another story. He ordered me to carry the luggage and follow him to a taxi. It wasn't much, my luggage, an average sized box which contained everything I owned; a pair of grey shorts for change, a couple of shirts, my high school certificates enclosed in an envelope, and some family and friends' photographs.

The taxi, a fifteen-seater omnibus, took ages to fill up before it sped up in the evening streets of Harare. Uncle Jokonya didn't miss the opportunity to sleep off some of the alcohol. I took the opportunity to observe my fellow passengers who didn't seem to mind being packed in the confined vehicle with other sweaty and smelly bodies.

A passenger sat next to me. She wasn't that much older than me. Probably with a child but still doing her studies. She restlessly flipped through a book, desperately trying to read the pages in the dimmed vehicle lights. I tried to peer on the leaves only to find names and numbers randomly written on every page. A phonebook, that's what it was. I quickly lost interest, I kept one eye on the book whilst the other looked in awe the night lights of Harare city.

Garden boy job (04) 404—

On her gravestone, my grandmother's date of birth was written as the fourth of April 1904. The same as the Garden boy job, whomever it was. It seemed like a job vacancy for a garden boy. I was certain I would have gotten the job if I had called. I instantly dropped the thought; I wasn't sure if the last digits were -34 or -43. Besides, I had passed with flying colours and was destined to get a clerical job or better.

***

I stayed with my uncle and his newest wife for three months in Kambuzuma. He would leave around 4 am and ride his bicycle to work in the CBD where he worked in a shoe factory. I would leave the house in the same direction only to spend the day roaming around the city looking for employment at every building I came across. We would meet home at around seven, have supper and retire to our beds. On my uncle's off days, I would ride his bicycle to the CBD. For three months, my life was a series of monotonous trips to find work.

I grew tired of the endless job search. I would go to the CBD, find a bench in Harare gardens, and sleep the day off. The flying colours I held close to my heart everyday grew heavy that I ended up reminding myself to forget them at home. It didn't change the situation anyhow. I was still unemployed. What I had was few coins my uncle gave me for 'emergencies'.

One day I took the coins, went to a pay phone booth, and dialed the garden boy job number.

Zero-four-four-zero-four-three-four.

The number was no longer in use. I loudly released a breath I didn't know I was holding. I could feel the wind cooling the sweat that had started to trickle down on my forehead.

Zero, four, four, zero, four, four, three.

I could hear the familiar sound of a ringing telephone on the other end of the line. It was utterly madness to beg employment from a stranger.

"Millstone residency, hello." A female voice came through the speaker.

"Good afternoon ma'am, I am looking for a job." I jabbered the half-baked thought on the microphone.

"This is a private residency and we don't have any open vacancy." She slammed the receiver down before I could thank her.

That day I spent my afternoon sleeping on the bench, dreaming what the woman on the other side of the telephone looked like. I could imagine her frowning at the telephone, telling whoever was beside her what a weird phone call she'd just received.

I hoped she was intrigued by our conversation as I had.

I went home early and was reimbursed the coins I had used to call her. All I had to do was tell my uncle it had been a necessary expense. He was half drunk and generous that night. He didn't think twice about my stupidity. I did not sleep soundly as one would expect after having a blissful day. I hit my head in shame as I remember how naive and clueless I had sounded on the phone. The conversation I had in my head sounded much better and my voice had much confidence of a grown-up man.

That night I dreamt of her, the woman on the other side of the telephone.

***

It was almost a week before I could garner enough courage to call her again. She answered after the third ring.

"Millstone residence hello," the perfect voice said, "Hello?"

I hadn't stocked up enough guts to say anything to her. I held on to receiver to my ear whilst a hundred or so thoughts ran in my mind.

"Milton, is that you?" She continued," I don't have much time Milton. I have to rush to the neighbourhood meeting. I haven't attended one in ages that some of the neighbours think I had already moved out of Mt Pleasant."

She erupted into a laugh before dropping the phone. I was left listening to the dialing tone. The payphone spitted some coins.

Change! The call had lasted less than a minute and I needed the coins for food. I promised myself never to call her again.

Mt Pleasant that was where she had said she lived. Millstone in Mt Pleasant. I doubted there were that many Millstones in Mt Pleasant. If I were to ask around that area I would find out where she lived exactly. It was no use though; I wasn't ever going to call her again, why bother knowing where she lived.

I had few hours to spare before going home. I had not found a job yet and my aunty was no longer excited to see me get back inside her home empty handed every day. I took the local telephone directory, they kept one inside the booth, and flipped the pages.

Millstone Morgan 275 Cecil Avenue Mt Pleasant 40443.

***

That night, when I told my uncle I had found a job at a car tyre dealer, he was in ecstasy. His breath smelt of booze although it was still a Monday night. I didn't ask questions; I knew he was dealing with a lot. His eyes had sunken further into his skull, I blamed my continuous dismal news of unemployment.

My aunt had already stopped talking to me. The pride she had shown whilst showing me to her neighbours was nowhere to be found. I couldn't tell if she had finally given in to the rumours that I was bewitched and destined to be poor and unemployed.

I was told to join my uncle as he garnished a huge calabash of homemade beer. I declined and told them how tired I was. I also told them I had to start preparation for my new job.

"Preparation? But you said you start in two weeks?" The mute aunty finally spoke.

It took me a minute or so to convince the couple it was normal. I listed a dozen procedures that were supposed to be done before I could be allowed to start work. I didn't know I was such a good liar.

"It's okay my nephew," my uncle said," if you need money or to use the bicycle in your preparations just tell me."

I nodded and went to bed. I dreamt of the woman at Millstone residence.

***

I couldn't continue going to town to call her. Fortunately, there was an old pay phone near the bus stop, a few yards from where we lived, and I used to call her from it. I decided to stick to a schedule, that way she would always answer, and her husband wouldn't.

"Hello Milton, I was thinking about you," she said before I could say anything, "Morgan went to the dentist today. He needed his replacements."

"I didn't have a clue how expensive it was. Well since we no longer have medical aid cover, we had to use our own savings. Lucas said he would help with some cash, but it seems business is not getting any better since he took over. "

It turned out that Morgan was her husband and Lucas her brother. Lucas had inherited the family business a year earlier when their father had abandoned it for England. He, the father, could not live in a country ruled by the blacks. He had been a high-ranking army man in the Rhodesian Patriotic Front. It made sense that he fled as soon as the war ended.

His son-in law, Morgan, had only risen to a rank of sergeant. He didn't come home with any medals or fortune. He had promised his then pregnant wife that they would leave for South Africa and buy a ranch or a farm.

"We'll leave as soon as we find the money," she sobbed a little, "if only he would stop spending all the money on at the casino."

She was telling me Morgan Millstone was a drunk, gambler and into prostitutes. She bade me goodbye; she had to be a good wife and cook supper for her husband.

***

Riding a bicycle from Kambuzuma to Mt Pleasant wasn't as easy as I had thought. The distance turned out to be thrice as long as I had anticipated. Halfway into the CBD I took off my jacket, it was soaking wet with sweat. The June breeze didn't help much.

After navigating the crowded city and the tricky streetlights systems, I easily slid to the low-density Mt Pleasant homes. It was quiet and peaceful.

The address system was quite confusing, and it took me an hour before I got the hang of it. Number 275 wasn't that hard to find after that. I slowly rode past as I closely looked at number 275.

It wasn't a house but a mansion. The building was a three-storey built on a large plot, large enough to be a sustainable maize field. It wasn't walled or fenced around; it was surrounded by flowers. There were flowers everywhere, all types of flowers and colours.

I tried to peer through the large windows, hoping to have just a glance of the madam. I wasn't lucky, the house looked locked and deserted. I sped up before anyone could suspect me of being a thief. I decided to come back the following day.

***

The following day I rode the bicycle to town. It was around 10 o'clock and I thought it was too early to go to Mt Pleasant and I decided to ride around the downtown a bit to pass time. That was when I saw it, Kaplan Hardware and Furniture, the perfect place I was deemed to find everlasting employment.

When I lived in the village, I was fond of reading and would go around asking neighbours for old newspapers and magazines. One neighbour had some to spare. Some of the magazines and newspapers were as old as my father. Somehow Kaplan hardware and furniture had already started selling wardrobes in the early 1920. It always fascinated me how such a business could run for so many decades. I used to imagine myself walk into one of their stores and buy a chair or table.

That day I got a chance to go into one of their stores. I left my bicycle chained to the lamp-post outside. The cleaner, a woman old enough to be my grandmother, welcomed me into the shop. I went straight to the white man who was sitting behind the counter. I politely asked for a job.

He wasn't pleased with me disturbing his newspaper reading time. My almost perfect English didn't impress him enough. I promised him I would bring a reference letter, my identification document, and my academic certificates the following day. He nodded and went back to reading his newspaper.

***

I went back the following day, with an ironed shirt and tie. The white man did not show up for work that day. The cleaning lady told me to wait and I waited the entire day. I didn't complain, I was now accustomed to the disappointments of the city. The cleaning lady was encouraging, she even shared her lunch with me and did not want me to leave with my certificate nor give them to her.

"I don't know how to read and write, and I am old and will lose them anytime. Give them straight into his hands and he hire you immediately." The old lady who said I reminded her of her grandson told me.

Around 4 pm I went home fed up and dejected. I didn't forget to pray for death to the white man who had me stood up.

***

Instead of going back to Kaplan Hardware and furniture the following day I decided to visit the Millstone residence again. A childish and a naive decision. My uncle and auntie believed that in about a week I would be starting a new job at a tire shop. A lie I even was starting to believe. I was still an unemployed youth with no prospects at all. It would have been an ideal decision if I'd gone to look for a job, I thought so as I rode my bicycle to Mt Pleasant.

As always, the streets were empty as I slowly came upon number 275. There was a deathly stench at the house and the yard was empty.

The yard wasn't empty, a fair skinned lady was crotched in the garden. She peered through the shrubs after noticing my presence. She stood up and I saw the garden fork in her hand. I looked away pretending not to see her.

I had seen enough. Her photograph had been captured in my memory. She looked to be in her late twenties. Grey eyes and perfectly small ears. She was donning a sky-blue dress which made her gracefully tall and slender. Not a single piece of jewellery was on her. I didn't have to imagine what her voice sounded like; it was the woman on the other end of the receiver.

I stopped my bike intending to go and talk to her. Halfway through the manoeuvre I changed my mind and tried to escape, I ended up falling to the ground. I quickly got back on the bicycle and sped away hoping that she at least felt sorry for me.

***

"Hello?" Her uncertain voice echoed from the other end of the receiver after I called her that afternoon, "Milton is that you?"

I grunted with pain from my bicycle accident, neither confirming nor declining the given name.

"A strange man is trying to rob our house," she said, her voice louder with excitement, "he passed by our house twice this week on a bicycle."

My heart skipped a bit. Fortunately, she didn't hear it. She went on to tell me how this young man, black as coal, had slowly cycled as he passed on her front yard. The lad had closely looked at her house, only her house, as if searching for something and had passed along. She was hidden in the garden, he didn't notice her. That was the first day.

"Then today he passed by again, "she continued with much vigour I hadn't heard from her for a long time, "He was wearing the same black hat, brown jacket and black trousers. He saw me forking my garden. For a moment I thought he was going to disembark from the bicycle and ask for a job. Then he changed his mind and sped off."

She did not say anything about the man giving the ground a hug and a kiss, I couldn't ask her.

She had grown accustomed to my silence that she didn't give me a time to speak. She promised me she would be safe and would use the gun her husband kept in the garage if the man ever came back again.

"Milton, do you think I should tell my husband about this man?" She asked and was answered only with my heavy breathing on the receiver.

"I won't tell him," her voice was filled with resignation, "he will think I am making it up just to have his attention. Or I am a weakling who also need his rescue at the first sign of trouble."

It was around five when she was done talking. She told me she had to go and prepare supper for her husband before he arrived from work. She dropped the receiver after she said her goodbye. She already knew there would be no answer from the other side of the phone.

***

When the rainy season came, my uncle and aunty sent me back to Buhera to help my parents with the ploughing and planting of the fields. My aunt promised me I would come back after harvesting was done. Of course, we all knew it was a lie. I had lied about getting a job and spent a lot of money on the payphone without anything in return. I agreed with their decision to send me home, I had to find my fortune elsewhere, the city of Harare was not the place.

On my day of departure, I decided to call her one last time. I had it all written down. I was going to tell my name; Milton was not my name and I didn't know where she got it from. I was going to tell her how much I loved her flower garden. I was going to ask her name. I was going to tell her all that was on my heart.

"Milton," she sobbed as soon as she picked the phone up, "Morgan is ill, he is in dire condition. Lucas and I are packing. We are all leaving this goddamned country. My father said he will help us settle in England. I don't want to go Milton, please help me."

I listened to her as she wept. My tongue tied and refusing to whisper a single word to smother her. I did nothing, just like as before.

This story was first published in The Rules of The City Anthology June 2021

The People Who Live Across the Highway

They, the people who live across the highway, drive fancy cars with weird names like Austin Martin or Maserati. They only keep those expensive machine on their side of the town. Probably because the northern side of the town, where they live, has the best roads and no potholes. Once, one of them drove a new Mercedes across the highway to the southern side of the town where the rest of us live. The car immediately got stuck in one of the thousand gullies on the road. The driver got out and asked us to help him. He was polite, well dressed and nice. He was great actually. The driver actually left us some money despite us leaving dirt and stains on his car after we pulled it out. The driver then got in the car and sped off to his kind of people.

The driver never drove his car again to our side of the highway. This memory probably scarred him. Our faces too, he never seemed to forget them. Every time he saw one of the dirty burgess who pulled him out of the gullies, he would hoot his Mercedes' or Ford Ranger's horn. We always waved back. At least he acknowledged our existence until he couldn't anymore. His was rich and nice.

He is not the only rich and nice person from across the highway. There are others too, like Madam Portia the widow (not her really name). No one from my side would ever dream of marrying a woman like her. It did not make sense either for a man to die leaving a beautiful woman like that. The people on my side of the highway whispered to each other that she was a widow by choice; that she had killed her husband for ritual purposes to make herself rich, but no, she is an angel; both in appearance and in heart. During the height of the lockdown caused by the pandemic, she opened a soup kitchen at her home. The people from my side of highway went there for their daily bread. Actually, the children did, the adults were too embarrassed to be seen scrambling for bread crumbs from her table. The soup kitchen did feed so many until the Councillor, armed with a cease and desist letter, made a stop of it. The Councilor was in company of the Officer in Charge of the Kaunda police station (note the name of the police station has been changed to protect the identity of individuals involved in this story) so everyone figured whatever Madam Portia was doing was illegal.

The Councilor also lives across the highway. We voted for him because we thought he was one of us, you know, from the southern side of the highway. His house is one of the mansions on the other side of highway although it is not the most beautiful nor the biggest on that side. Every house on that side is better than the last. The houses are surrounded by huge walls with electric wires on top. Not only are the roads tarred but they are spotless clean. The Councilor makes sure that refuse is collected twice a week on that side. The Councilor forgets to send the garbage truck to our side of the town. Uncollected rubbish and free flowing sewage are the only things that surrounds the shacks that are our homes. The Councilor isn't that much of a bad person though, he is known to be vehemently open about drug abuse on our side of the highway. He even opened a clinic for the addicts, although it was said that he financed it from the money he got after killing his business partner. The clinic was a success even Reverend K got involved in supporting its cause.

Reverend K of The Miracle Grace Baptist Family Church of the new light of Mercy and Glory Ministries is one of the few people who like the people from southern side of the town to cross the highway and come to his church. Not only does he provide spiritual guidance and demon deliverance on Sundays, Reverend K also teaches necessary technical skills to his parishioners. It is there that he spends quality time with his mistress, rumour has it. It is believed that the affair has been going on for a long time that his wife acknowledges it. The wife claims that her husband killed one of his congregate in order to have his wife as his mistress. But then, the Reverend is holy and pure. He even pays school fees and tuition for youth in our side of the highway. Youths who would have ended up being locked up by the sturdy Officer in Charge at the Kaunda police station.

No one knows exactly how much an officer in charge earns but the big house he bought on the other side of the highway says a lot. Then, he is a civil servant he can't afford that house. Unless he is corrupt. The Officer in Charge of Kaunda Police station is corrupt. He arrest youths from the southern side of the highway whilst the killers who live on the other side of the highway are left free because they are rich and nice. On his first month in office, a man who live on the other side of the highway was found murdered. The Officer send his subordinates scrambling for answers and they did find them. However the suspect offered the poor government official an enormous amount of money for the entire thing to go away. No one from our side of the highway can afford to pay off an officer in charge, so it must be someone from the other side of the highway. The hush money worked, since then no one ever mentions the murdered man's name, Herbert G-.

Herbert G- was a husband, business man, devoted Christian, and a law abiding citizen. His wife was devastated when his lifeless body was found in the street. Madam Portia vowed to be a philanthropist because that's what her husband would have wanted her to do, whatever that was. His business partner, the Councilor, wrote a long letter and posted it on a billboard along the highway. The Councilor renamed a road on the other side of the highway in honour of his business partner. Reverend K had an entire sermon dedicated to him. He had known the man since he opened his church, he was an exemplary church member. The Rev appointed the man's wife a deacon and promised to help her fulfill her husband's wishes. The Officer in Charge talked about it in the community Hall. He vowed to bring the perpetrators to Justice. He had known the man for few weeks and had seen the perfect model of how a citizen should live. Amongst the lot, he sounded the most Ernest

Apparently Herbert G- was also lousy and noisy driver too. He used to hoot his car horn whenever he saw a group of ragged people from the southern side of the highway. Maybe that was because he remembered the help they gave him when he drove his car to that side of the highway and got stuck in a porthole the size of a swimming pool. No one knows what happened to Herbert G- but the people from our side of the highway are sure it has something to do with the people who live on the other side of the highway.

Incognito

You are no longer a toddler, you are eight or maybe nine, and no one keeps precise records. Anyways, your parents treat you like a toddler because you are their last child and their only son. You are not their only last child though; you have a sister, a twin. You don't like her much; she has been fighting with you, even when you were still in your mother's womb.

"Boy!" Your older sister yells at you, "Stop fighting with your sister."

The three of you are coming from church, it's a late afternoon on a Sunday. You have left the rest of the family talking to the pastor. The pastor is new in the village and your mother thought it wise to introduce her five unmarried daughters to him. Your older sister, the one you are walking home with, is still too young to get a husband and she was sent home along with you toddlers.

"Boy!" She yells again, "I told you to stop hitting your sister!"

"She started it first. You tell her."

"No, I didn't!" Your twin sister interjects, "He is the one pushing me out of the road."

It's not a road it's just a well-trodden footpath. There is no single road in the village. There are dozens of them, footpaths, connecting hundreds of huts in the village. It's an old village hundreds of kilometres from the nearest town. The bus only comes once a week from the city. The nearest school is in another village, five kilometres away. Not that it matters much to you but the only man who has a wireless radio in the village is not your father and at your age you are yet to see the magic called electricity.

"Girl stop nagging your brother now," your older sister screams somewhere behind you, "and apologise to him now!"

Your foe shakes her head, refusing to be defeated in that manner. She is short, dark skinned and as thin as a stick. She has black hair and is donning a plain blue dress. She is bare footed; your parents can't afford to buy shoes for you all.

"He started it," your twin starts, "I won't apologise to him."

You are angry at the disrespect your sister flanges at you. She doesn't listen to what your mother says, about you being their only brother and will be her father-figure when your own father passes on. All those Sunday school bible teachings about her submitting to man are stupid to her. You are terribly angry at her.

"Boy come back here!" Your older sister demands, "Where do you think you are going?"

You don't answer her or turn around; you continue your way off the footpath into the bushes. You decide to go to the kopje and cool off or else you might end up hitting your twin. You don't like hitting her, your mother told you never to hit women.

The kopje is where you and other boys of your age hang around when you have done your house chores. It's quite and far from the village. On the kopje you can see the entire village, all the way from the grocery store to the billboard. The billboard is next to the river. The White men put up the billboard and wrote that they were going to turn the river into a reservoir in March of 1967. You can't read or write; it was your sister who told you what was written on the board.

There is no one at the kopje. You expected it anyways, your gang doesn't hang around on Sundays. After church no one is allowed to be seen roaming around the village. It's a rule every parent gives their child for no good reason at all. You sit by yourself and watch the sun dip its toes into the earth.

You don't want to arrive late, so you spring up and head home. You decide to take a shortcut, the one that pass through your neighbour's orchard. Your neighbour has the finest banana trees in the whole village, it would be wrong not to pluck a couple and eat them on your way home.

"Boy?"

You are startled by the hesitant feminine voice. You slowly turn around. It's not the owner of the orchard, you are relieved a bit, but you don't know who she is.

"Boy is that really you?" the girl asks taking a step towards you. You take a step back. You don't know her although she looks familiar. She is a teenager and looks like any one of your seven sisters. You know your sisters well, but she is not your sister. You turn and start running away. You only glance once to see her running towards your own homestead. You realize then that's what you should have done, run home not back to the kopje.

You sit on the kopje, mesmerised by the beauty of the cloudless sky. You have gazed at the stars a hundred nights before but on this night the constellations call to you. You huddle between rocks and try to sleep but the face of the girl who tried to capture you haunts your mind. You don't think much about the reason she ran to your homestead, maybe to wait for you there?

It's morning; you don't remember when you dosed off. It was maybe during your prayer to God from church or maybe when you were begging your ancestors to protect you from the chilly night, but morning is finally upon you. You have to rush home or else your mother will be worried. She is already worried, you know that, but she might be easily persuaded to give you fewer lashes if you were to arrive home early. This is not your first time not sleeping home, you already know the drill.

You rush down to the river to wash your face. You are still in your Sunday clothes and it's better you arrive home presentable. You wash your face in the chilly waters and start making your way home. You see your mother coming down to the river, there is a yellow bucket in her hand. She sees you coming from the riverbank.

"Boy?" The woman who looks like your mother asks, "is that you Boy?"

You don't know this woman, she might be your mother's sister or relative, but you have already been warned by your parents not to talk to strangers. You flee from the mad woman screaming your name. You run through the orchard towards your home. You only took a quick look in the orchard to see if the teenage girl from the previous night is still there. If she finds you, you are afraid she will not let you go home.

You see her picking up green mangoes. A sigh of relief escapes your mouth, it's not the girl but an old woman. She is probably one of the wanderers who begs for food on their way to nowhere, you are not sure.

"Will you help me here my grandson?" She calls to you. You move closer to help her; you feel pity for her. You pick a couple of mangoes and place them into her plastic bag.

"Help me to sit on the ground young man." She commands you and you follow. "I have waited for this moment for a long time Boy."

You look at the old woman who calls you by name. She looks familiar but you can't place her. You don't know what to make of her.

"I knew you would come back again Boy to see me before I die."
The Old woman sobs. You are confused.

****

Few days after her mother's burial Santa was sitting under the
avocado tree shade in the late afternoon when she saw a stranger
walk towards the house. The stranger did not do the customary
wailing for the dead as expected of her, she just walked up to the gate
and knocked. Santa stood up and dragged her feet to open the gate
for the stranger. Although she was in her fifties, Santa could feel old
age taking hold in her bones. How could she not look old, she had
borne twelve sons in her prime.

The visitor who was at the gate looked out of place. She wore a
pink dress and high heels, like the one the school mistresses wore.
She was definitely not from the village. No one from the village wore
heels to walk in the muddy and cow dung infested streets. The visitor
looked young, maybe thirty, but Santa wasn't sure; pretty dressed
people always look young.

"Sisi Santa it's me Rujeko," the stranger peering at the gate said,
"I have come back home."

Santa opened the gate for her younger sister and gave her a hug.
She smelt unfamiliar and foreign, the way someone new smelt like.
She was like a stranger after all, Rujeko hadn't been home in twenty
years. Last time Santa had seen her younger sister, Rujeko was still a
teenager. It was few days after their father had died, Rujeko had an
episode. She left home days later when everybody on the village
coerced their mother to take Rujeko to a nearby Witchdoctor who
would treat Rujeko's mind.

Between the hugging, tears fell, and mouths blabbed how they had missed each other.

"If only you had come earlier," Santa said under her breathe. She wasn't about to start a fight with a sister she hadn't seen in decades, "if only you had come back a week earlier to ask for mother's forgiveness before she had died."

"How is the rest of our sisters?" Rujeko asked after condolences had been passed back and forth.

"They are happy and in good health." Santa lied. Santa wasn't sure if Rujeko could take the crushing disappointment and anger of her other five older sisters. Santa had always known Rujeko as the bullied youngest daughter. Despite Santa being only two years older than her, they seemed not family.

"We have a lot to talk about but first let me go to the river and fetch bathing water, I had a long journey from the city." Rujeko said as she grabbed a bucket and made her way to the river. The river wasn't far, maybe a hundred yards or so from the house.

Santa sat down under the tree again. Her gaze was fixed on Rujeko who was making her way to the river, with a yellow bucket in hand. The river was downhill; however, the bank was covered with the shrubs and tall grass. The moment her sister disappeared out of sight; Santa started wondering how she would tell her prodigal sister that their mother had left the house to Rujeko. In way she was thrilled to have her back, however a lingering fear of losing her again made her tread carefully on what she would talk to her about.

Before she had time to settle on her thoughts, Santa saw a mad woman running from the direction Rujeko disappeared to. No, it wasn't just a random mad woman. It was Rujeko racing along with the wind back to the homestead.

Santa took a quick glance in the neighbours' house to see if anyone were out and about to witness the spectacle. Fortunately, the September scorching sun overhead had kept everyone indoors.

"Sisi Santa, come and see quickly!" she shouted as she approached the gates

"What is it Rujeko?"

"I saw him." The words came out between her breathes." I saw Ranganai washing his face in the river."

"Don't do this again."

"It's true sisi!" Rujeko begged.

"Please don't."

Once upon a time the two sisters had had a brother. He was Rujeko's twin. Ranganai was his name. The two were close, a special bond that the rest of the family could not understand. One Sunday afternoon when the trio, Santa, Ranganai and Rujeko, was coming from church Ranganai disappeared into the woods and was never to be seen nor heard from again. The whole family was devastated, Rujeko took it the hardest, more than their own mother.

After five years of searching to no avail, their father gave up and died. He left an already grieving wife and seven daughters. Few days after they buried their father; Rujeko who was fetching some mangoes from their neighbour's orchard, came back home screaming and shouting that she had seen Ranganai picking bananas in the same orchard. The family accompanied by half of the village went to search. They found nothing, not even a footprint. Rujeko was punished severely, their mother wasn't allowed to let her go freely. Rujeko insisted that it was not a prank, no one believed her. Some village elders encouraged their mother to seek help from a witch doctor who was an expert in diseases of the mind. Rujeko begged their mother to

45

believe her, but she looked the other way. Rujeko then packed her things and left.

"Rujeko, please don't do this." Santa asked again.

Santa could see her sister slumbering on the gate, desperately wanted to be believed in. It didn't matter, she wanted Rujeko to stay. Santa lied to her, convinced her to stay, and whispered in to Rujeko's ears that the ghost of their lost brother wanted to visit her at their birth home.

This story first appeared in libretto Magazine issue 7 in June 2022

Plastic lives

She wakes up in the middle of the night to faint sounds coming through the thin walls -muffled baby cries. There's a baby next door. She sits on the bed, under the warm blankets, and listens to it whine for its mother. She strains her ears, desperate to hear the mother sing the baby back to sleep. She closes her eyes, patiently waits for the silence. The crying doesn't stop for hours.

The crying suddenly stops. She opens her eyes to see the sky turning yellow through the window. Finally, sunrise. She looks around the room - it's lavishly furnished. There are only clothes and things that might belong to her, they are hers. She has slept alone on the bed. There's only her presence in the room. She is alone. She has never been alone before, not even once in her past lives.

In her past life, the one she was in before waking up to the sound of muffled baby cries, she was a housewife. The husband worked nights maybe that is the reason she is unable to sleep with muffled baby cries disturbing the night. She is accustomed to silence. Not the loneliness though, the husband in her previous life had loved her all the time they were both awake. In this life she doesn't have a husband, only a neighbour's baby who had kept her awake on her first night.

She puts on a robe and goes out. She knocks on the neighbour's door. She continues to bang the door for ten more minutes. No one answers. She wonders if the neighbours are busy with the baby or if they are still sleeping because the baby kept them awake the whole night. She doesn't know her neighbours yet and doesn't want to impose yet, so she abandons her quest and goes back to her house.

She sleeps on her own bed and dreams about her past lives, all eight of them. She dreams of them, or maybe relives the memory of them, she is not sure of which the two is happening. Then something is misplaced; there is a crying baby in one of her previous life. It is in her fourth, the one she worked at a brothel. The crying baby drowns out the sweet music she swerves to in the nude. She wakes up oozing of sweat and confusion. She hears the baby wailing in her neighbour's home. She listens and patiently waits for its parent to smoother it.

The neighbours fail to keep the baby quiet. She gets out of the bed and goes back to the neighbour's door. She hammers the door with her fists but the baby screams even louder than her knocking. The noise is already causing her a headache, if the baby continues crying, her head is going to crack open. She pounds the door harder, her life depends upon it. Her knuckles gets bruised.

She remembers bruises on her knuckles. In fact, she remembers bruises all over her body and her head cracking open. She remembers the crying and the wailing of her siblings. It was in another life where her father used to beat the lights out of her and the rest of the family. She can't stand it, the wailing of the child. She has to get into the neighbours house, the child needs her.

Her neighbour's door is not locked. She nudges it open and hesitantly walks in. The house is furnished the same as hers. It is identical to hers except for one thing; a crying baby in a cot. She looks around for the owner of the baby. No, the caregiver of the child. There is no one else in the house. It's not abandoned though - there's a kettle on the stove. No one would abandon such a little pretty thing. The baby is beautiful, like a flower. Not just any flower but a daffodil.

Daffodil. Her most memorable past life was spent in a garden. An entire summer of sun and moist ground. Weeks of dancing in the wind. It was also her shortest life; when she was at the peak of blossoming and blooming, she was plucked out with the other daffodils. Her entire lifetime in a vase come to end because someone envied her beautiful yellow petals. She was a beautiful flower in her fifth life. She had learnt that beautiful things don't last.

The beautiful baby can't last without her. She picks it up but it doesn't stop crying. She puts it back in the cot and starts ransacking the house for diapers. She finds them neatly packed in a cardboard. She quickly takes one and rushes back to the baby. She changes the baby's diaper on the kitchen table. She dumps the dirty diaper in the sink. She takes the baby back to the cot and waits for it to sleep. It gazes back at her with dark mesmerizing eyes. She rocks the cot. She doesn't know any lullabies so she sings the sweet songs she learnt in her fourth life, the one she worked in a brothel.

Her voice starts to croak. She has been singing for hours and it's not good for her throat. Fortunately, the baby finally closes its eyes and naps. She looks around the house and is astonished by the mess she has made. She decides not to clean it up. Her neighbours will clean it when they return. She wonders where the neighbours have gone for hours ends leaving the baby all alone. She has taken care of the baby, the neighbors will take care of the rest.

She walks slowly back to her own house. Her neighbour's baby has drained every ounce of energy in her. She goes straight to her bedroom and throws herself on the bed. Too tired to go under the sheets. She starts to doze off. She stretches her hand for the husband. She remembers the husband isn't here, she left him in her eighth life.

She misses him and wonders what her life would have been like had she continued to play housewife.

She hopes, when she wakes up again, this life will be over and the ringing in her ears of the wailing baby would be a faint memory of a sound, whose source and meaning she will never recall. She envision her tenth life exciting, she being a someone of importance or something. She dreams her next life filled with peace. She wills for a miracle; an escape to another life that she knows she is destined for. As she sleeps, she remembers her past lives, all nine of them. She doesn't like her ninth life but she dreams it anyway with nurseries and rhymes.

The sound of a whimpering child rouse her from her slumber. Her house is dark but she can see moonlight flooding through the window. She is still in the same bedroom she sleeps in. It is still the same baby next door crying for attention. She gets out of the bed, puts on a slippers and makes her way out of her house straight to her neighbour's front door.

She softly knocks on the door. The crying is louder than the knocking. She pushes the door ajar. The room is well lit. The baby is in its cot but there's no one else in the house. She looks in the other rooms and notices the mess she left earlier is gone. Someone cleaned it up. She takes the baby out of the cot and start singing to it. The cries don't recede. She knows if she continues hearing the baby's cry her head will explode. She starts praying.

Pray. That was the only thing she had done in her second life. That life had abruptly begun with her vomiting on the side of the road. She couldn't remember how her first one had ended, she chose not to remember. After throwing up, she picked herself up and went straight to a church. She didn't recognize who she was but most

50

importantly she needed to know what she had become. The church didn't have the answers for her. Neither did she find the answers in a mosque, nor a temple nor a synagogue. She spent her second life praying every day from one deity to another.

It is the same interwoven prayer she says to make the baby quiet or at least for the return of its parent. She tells the baby stories about her past lives. The baby stops crying as if captivated by the tale of her third life, where she played with her siblings during the day waiting for their father to come home in the evening and beat them near to death.

The baby is soundly asleep. She sits beside the cot. She has to wait with the baby until its parent returns. She sleeps soundly besides the baby. For the first time in this life, she feels her body rest.

She wakes up screaming. A nightmare of a life lived, her sixth. It's the one with all the dead bodies in it. She tries to forget it but it is all that now she can think of. She looks at the baby which is sound and peacefully asleep. She sees the sun starting to rise. She wonders what happened to the baby's parent. Soon the baby will wake up, it will be hungry and it will cry. If the baby cries again, she knows that's will be the end of her.

She starts rummaging through the house again. She opens every cardboard, cabinet, drawer and even the wardrobe in search of baby food. Most of these compartments are empty as if no one lives in the house. She finds nothing and the house is now in disarray. She starts putting everything back in to order. She wipes the dirty on the shelves and mops the floor. She vacuums the carpet and fold the baby's laundry. The house is spotless clean and homely for the baby.

She has done it before - the cleaning and putting back to order - in her sixth life. In that life she had sewn together body parts of children and women who were gutted in a war they were never part of. She had tried to clean herself off that life but it was in her and wouldn't wash off with just soap and water.

She trudges to the bathroom. There she takes off her clothes. She gets into the shower and turns on the cold water. Cold water always reminds her of the life she is living. In the shower she tries to scrub herself clean from this life but fails. She dries herself and walks to her neighbour's bedroom and opens the wardrobe. There she takes out some stranger's clothes, shoes and underwear. She wears them. They do not fit nor are they comfortable. She stands in front of a mirror not sure of this life.

Then the baby wakes up and starts crying in its cot. She rushes to pick it up and pretends to throw it in the air. The baby loves it and it giggles happily in her arms. She takes out her left breast and put it on the baby's mouth. The baby starts suckling, content with just existing. The baby worries nothing and this worries her. She continues feeding the baby, waiting for it to sleep so that she too can sleep and dream. Dream about her past lives, all nine of them.

The Exorcist

Someone splashes icy water on your face. You open your eyes again. You are still sitting on the dirt and tied to the small tree. You father is kneeling few yards away on your right. Once in a while he casually cast a nervous glance in your direction. You know exactly what he thinks of you.

You don't know exactly what to make of the man pacing forth and back in front of you. He is the one who poured water on you. He is huge, bald, and probably the darkest of men you have ever seen. For a second, just a second, you wonder how it would feel to bear him sons. You quickly push the thought away from your mind. It is not appropriate to have naughty thoughts for a man of God who is trying to save you.

The man of God walks slow towards the tree, the one you are tied on with loose rope, and pluck a small twig. His huge and once white garment drag dirt in his wake. He is bare footed; you are on his holy shrine after all. You can smell his unwashed body from three feet away.

"I command you to tell me, who you are!" The holy man barks in your ear.

"It's me Naledi." you tell him for the third time.

The man shakes his head and walks towards your father. You can hear him whispering in your father's ears, "The demon possessing your daughter is immensely powerful. I need permission to use my special technique to exorcise it."

Your father consents. The dark man returns with fury in his eyes and the small twig in hand. The situation is getting ridiculous.

"Who are you?" He bellows again. Before you can answer he hit your face with the twig. A tingle of pain rip through your face and you can feel a couple of teardrops roll down on your cheek. "Why have you taken possession of this young woman's body?"

You don't answer. Either way you were going to get hit again in the face. You look at your father with a plea on your face. He looks more scared than you.

The man in the huge garment is in control now.

"Tell me demon who are you?" He is louder now, "I know you are hiding in her. You are the one who is causing her to refuse to get married."

You preferred to finish your diploma in education before you are married off to someone you don't know. You know it's not a demon but you. You know what he will say next; the demon is responsible for you quitting church. You know the demon was the church bishop who wanted you to be his third wife. Besides you have always found comfort and peace in the way of your ancestors than the white dead man hung in the church.

"Demon show yourself!" The man of God is oozing with sweat now.

You are Naledi! You are Naledi right? Or maybe you are the demon. Who are you? You don't know. A slap on the cheek brings you back from your own thoughts. You glance in your father's direction to see his face beaming with expectation. He will probably give the man of God a hen for his service in getting rid of you or the demon in you, you can't tell the difference between the two yet.

"I think it's working!" Your father ejaculate from the other side of the shrine.

"Yes, it is, but we have to know its name before I can send it to gates of hell where the other demons are!" The holy man says, "I will ask again, who are you?"

Is it because you are one of the few in the village who still want to appease and seek guidance from your ancestors that you are made to suffer like that? No, you are a Zezuru and you know what your ancestors are to you.

"I will ask again, who are you?"

You look at your father then at the man of cloth. You want to answer. You don't know the answer. Are you Naledi or the demon? You don't know, who are you?

This story first appeared in Con-Scio Magazine issue 2 volume 1 in July 2022

A Little Song for the Young One

She didn't have to look at her wristwatch to know she was going to be late to work, again. The previous week her youthful employer had let it slid but she knew this time it wasn't going to be that easy. She tried to quicken her pace, it didn't help much, she was old and slow. Fifty-three years old, that wasn't young at all.

Quarter to six. It was almost dark, and the streets were getting empty. It was good, the darkness got rid of the smelly and unwashed bodies that roamed freely in the streets of Durban. She preferred to walk in the evening breeze on her way to work, in peace and silence whilst enveloped in her own dark thoughts.

"Salibonani, Mama Zodwa!" A man from a banana stall greeted her as she passed. She raised her hand and waved at him, she didn't have enough time to return a proper greeting and to chat. Besides if she were to greet everyone she knew, she wouldn't ever arrive at her destination. She knew everyone in the city, well, almost everyone in the city. She had been born here. At thirteen Mama Zodwa had started working as a maid, nanny and a laundry lady. Heck, she even delivered fresh milk to hundreds of people who lived in the eastern side of Durban. It wasn't a wonder that everyone knew her, and a lot of people offered her jobs. She only accepted those job offers if children happened to be involved.

Despite the September evening being warm Mama Zodwa donned a long brown and black dress, a wrapping towel was thrown over her shoulders and her grey hair was uncovered, short and well-trimmed. On her feet she wore knee-length black socks and high heels shoes which made a clacking sound on the paved driveway as she arrived at her workplace.

She found Ms. Pete impatiently tapping the door handle, waiting for her arrival. Ms. Pete was young, twenty-five maybe, and was from Greece. It might not be the reason why her kind of dressing was weird; a strapless tiny blouse, mini-skirt, and high heels all in black. It was this kind of revealing clothes she left wearing those Thursday evening when she hired Mama Zodwa to stay over for the night with her seven-year-old son, Jeremy.

"You are late," Ms. Pete said grabbing her handbag and keys, "next time I want to be so forgiving."

She didn't wait for Mama Zodwa to reply before dashing out to the driveway where her car was parked. Mama Zodwa's greeting was left on her lips.

"She's definitely a prostitute," Mama Zodwa said murmured to herself as she made her way to Jeremy's bedroom, "or else how would she afford this luxurious house."

Jeremy was reading his favourite storybook, about cows, giants, and a boy, whilst he lay on his tiny bed. He looked up as Mama Zodwa bulged in the boy's room without knocking. A minute smile tried to form on his lip, but it died without reaching his grey eyes. He was already in his pajamas. Jeremy was a chubby and an unhappy boy.

Mama Zodwa took out a lunchbox of mashed potatoes and gave it to the boy in silence. On numerous occasions, Ms. Pete had forgotten to feed his son before she left to work on those Thursday nights. Mama Zodwa wasn't sure if that evening was one of them, it was confirmed seconds later when the boy garnished the contents of the lunchbox with his bare hands. Half a minute later he was laying on the bed staring on the ceiling with a satisfied look on his face.

"Will you tell me the story of the fisherman again before I sleep, Mama Zodwa?"

"No dear, tonight I will sing for you one of my favourite folklore song my grandmother taught me but first let me go and lock up and do the dishes." She replied with her smothering motherly voice.

The boy gave a small smile as Mama Zodwa left the room for the kitchen, she found it in disarray. Pots and pans on the floor. Plates and spoons, from last week's lunch with the priest, were stashed in the sink and under the table. Mama Zodwa cursed before she started washing them.

She thought to herself how it would be nice to have such money and a beautiful home like Ms. Pete's. She didn't know what Ms. Pete did for a living but what she knew was; that every Thursday evening Mama Zodwa was called upon to babysit Jeremy for the whole night. Ms. Pete would leave wearing fancy clothes only to return the next morning still looking fresh and young. Without saying any word Ms. Pete would hand her a couple of two hundred Rand notes, Mama Zodwa would accept them and take her leave without questions. It still would be nice if she could afford those fancy things and food like her employer. Surely with all this money Mama Zodwa would finally be able to afford a doctor who would treat her aliment properly.

She was old, sick, and dying.

A strange curse was coursing through her veins, causing her pain and temporary paralysis. Since birth, Mama Zodwa had suffered from such disease that no witchdoctor had been able to cure her. She did found relief in children though, a little lick or suck of the young one's blood restored her healthy, just for a couple of days though, but it was enough to call a life.

After washing the dishes, Mama Zodwa cleaned the kitchen and went back to Jeremy's room. He was still awake, waiting for his favourite nanny.

Mama tucked him in and lay beside him on the tiny bed. Jeremy didn't have to beg twice before Mama Zodwa started to sing to him. It might have been a hymn, it might have been a chant, the difference between the lyrics and the incarnations were lost to the little boy who drowsed to the feminine voice which sliced the night with its Zulu enchantments. It was no ordinary folklore, Mama Zodwa knew of its magic.

Few minutes later it had done its job; Jeremy, who was now half asleep, grabbed Mama Zodwa's hand and begged her not to leave his side. From the trance he murmured something about a kiss on the forehead and how it would help him sleep better. Mama hesitated for a second, a tingle of guilty ripped from her heart before she savagely kissed him until a drop of blood fell. She licked it and decided to take the opportunity to live a little longer. She put her mouth back on the tiny wound, sucked a little more blood. She couldn't resist. She sucked some more; she did not let go until the sun came up.

This story first appeared in Zimbolicious volume 7 in 2023

Housekeeping

Seventy-five years. That was how long Maud had stayed inside the house, not even once leaving its doors to enjoy a little sunshine. Her shoulders had become slumped; she couldn't tell weather from old age or the repetition of scrubbing and dusting the big house spotless clean each and every day of those seventy-five years. Maybe it was the weight she carried on her shoulders that made her back slouch; the weight of a slimy green worm that had ate bits of her soul for many decades.

Maud walked down the stairs, each step she descend accompanied by a loud breath and cracking of bones. A couple of steps down she could feel her knees ready to buckle. If her own legs failed her at that moment, she would tumble down the stairs to her death. The visitor, she had been waiting for, would find her a few hours later and would not understand her purpose. She continued to climb the stairs as meticulous as ever.

Halfway down the stairs was a tiny window that overlooked the fields and dust road outside. When she reached it she decided to take a rest. Maud stared at the window hoping to catch a glimpse of the reflection of the weight on her shoulders but it was futile. She had done an excellent job of cleaning the glass window that not a sparkle of dirt remained. The glass was so clear that Maud could see dust raised a kilometer or so down the road which led straight to the house. Dust on the road meant travellers- that meant her visitor would arrive soon.

She slowly reached downstairs without further trouble. She walked slowly to the sitting room mentally debating herself weather she still had time to take a nap before her visitor arrived or wait at the door. She decided the former. Maud made her way to the century old armchair, and comfortable, relaxed on it. Everything in the house was old, half a century at least. The most recent item in the house was a rotary phone which Maud had helped install in the first decade of her tenure as the housekeeper. Maud closed her eyes and remembered that day she last had had visitors. Before she had doze off, the doorbell chimed. Her visitor had arrived.

A girl with fake blue hair walked in.

That wasn't how Maud had imagined her visitor to look. She had expected a young woman with short black hair or a cloth wrapping around her hair, maybe with a thick layer of makeup to cover bruises her husband inflicted on her. Maud didn't hope this girl had a husband or boyfriend she was running away from, no, but if you had to come to the house you had to be running away from something. The teenage who had walked on was free, happy, and not old in enough to carry the weight of the house on her shoulders.

"Wow, I just went back in time," the girl said," Is this like an antique store or a museum? Do you know how much money you can make by selling all this old stuff online?"

Maud didn't know what the girl meant. It didn't matter though, if the girl was the one, then Maud had to start training her before it was too late. Maud's own time was now limited, her soul was almost finished, drained by the weight of the house on her shoulders. She asked the girl if she knew why she was at the house.

"I know why I am here old lady. The Ad said it was a house, man, this is a mansion! Am I supposed to clean it all by myself?" The girl asked.

"You can stay in this house for the rest of your life but you will have to clean it each and every day." Maud told the newcomer." If you can't live in this house for the rest of your life now is the time to go back wherever you come from."

"I can't go back," the girl said in a small voice, "I have nowhere else to be except here. I will do everything you ask."

Maud smiled. That was the answer she needed. Everything else would fall in to place now that she had a successor. She said, "Good, if you learn the rules of the house, keep it clean, and be able to bear the weight of the house on your shoulders, I will leave you the house when I die."

The girl gaped, the surprise of owning a mansion too great to keep her mouth tight. She quickly grabbed an apron and started searching for something to do in the room. Maud was impressed with the girl's eagerness to please. Decades earlier, she had been where the girl was; running around the house doing whatever it takes to woo the then housekeeper to leave her the house. She kept its rules, kept it clean and the house was hers after the passing of the housekeeper. The weight of the house that later fell on her shoulders wasn't what she expected, her predecessor had never actually mentioned what it actually was.

"What is your name, girl?" Maud asked.

"Saru," the girl with blue hair said," My name is Sarudzai."

***

Sarudzai patiently waited at the door for the knock promised. She knew it was finally the day her visitor would arrive. She was prepared. Sarudzai wondered if that was what her predecessor had done on Sarudzai's own arrival. Sarudzai tried to recall the former housekeeper's name, Maud, but her face was lost in Sarudzai's mind.

That was half a century ago when she had last seen Maud's face, a long time she had never seen another face.

Her own successor would come soon. Sarudzai wasn't going to hide anything to the new arrival; she could keep the house but she had to let a green worm suck her soul until she died.

The former housekeeper had called it the weight of the house. Sarudzai scoffed at the name befitting the monster on her shoulders. If she wasn't distracted that day with the prospect of owning a mansion she could have noticed what she was getting into. Her greed had overcame her.

Sarudzai glanced at the clock, it was almost seven in the evening. She hoped her visitor was late not cancelling. She had done enough cleaning and now hoped for death. Her heart lept as someone knocked on the door. Her visitor had arrived.

A Special Place

Two years after the Chimurenga war ended my older sister, Tilda, came back home. It was the seventh year since she had sneaked away from the house during a November stormy night. My mother had started believing that, somehow, she had found a way to join the freedom fighters across the border in Mozambique, and by the grace of the Lord, she had perished together with thousands of other young people fighting for the liberation of Zimbabwe. It was a lie of course, she didn't want to believe what my father said was a disgrace to the family; Tilda, the daughter of a strict village pastor and his wife who was a primary school headmistress, had ran away to Salisbury to indulge in wantonness and debaucheries only offered by the city. Well it didn't matter much though; she had finally come back home. She didn't come along alone though, a six-year-old boy was in her tow.

My parents said they couldn't accept a bastard in their home, my parents said.

In a way they were right, Takura, for that was his name, was not ours to keep but his father's family. My father could not fathom the idea of keeping his daughter's embarrassment for the world to sneer and laugh at, that would have been rubbing salt to a fresh wound. I couldn't imagine what would happen to the pastor's famous anti-fornication preaching in the village, if the pastor's own daughter could not follow them it then who would? Before she had even unpacked her bags, the pastor was ready to kick her outside out of his house. Tilda sobbed.

In their scaling of their daughter's morality they almost left out the most important thing; Takura was their grandson and my nephew too. His father might have been one of the countless men my sister associated with at the shebeen she worked at in the city or maybe one of the boys who had ran run away to die in the war, my sister wasn't sure. She was a whore who would burn in hell, my mother did not mince her words. Tilda wept.

Shedding tears for the plight of her child was something that made me believe Tilda genuinely loved her son and it struck my eyes and my mother's heart. The headmistress would not sit and watch her daughter kneeling on the ground waiting for whatever life was about to through throw at her. She joined her daughter in rolling in the mud begging the Lord's servant to soften his stance. The husband loved the wife too much to refuse her of anything, he agreed for the sinner to sleep in the house for the night until a permanent solution could be found the following day. Tilda then left the following day.

Unlike the first time, she had the courtesy of leaving a note explaining that she had been called back to work at and she would come back in a few days to see her son. A 'few days' turned into a few weeks and my parents were already planning to go to the city and dump the little brat wherever its mother was participating in promiscuous behaviour. Before they could pack it off, they took a final look at the boy. Although he wore oversized khaki shorts and no shoes, it was apparent that he was the fragile type, so thin that he would shatter if squeezed too hard. His well-patched and even torn shirt exposed his smooth and handsomely dark skin. That was his only clothes. His huge long black hair added an inch to his short height. His tiny nose and ears matching his small mouth with an adorable huge smile. And his eyes, sometimes I wonder if they only kept him because of his eyes.

At six Takura had neither seen the comeliness of moon nor the horror or the summer sun. His eyes could open but all what he has endured since birth was darkness. Unlike some children of his age, colours were a myth to him and the beauty of the night sky a legend to his pretty little ears. Takura's mother had never said anything about his blindness, she had just pretended that everything was well, but I knew my sister, it must have been tiring to ignore the difference.

The first thing I ever gave him was a walking stick. I picked up a perfectly straight wooden stick along the road, tied a tiny steel metal on one end and some cloth on the other end to make a comfortable handle. I didn't know if it was of any use but every person with visual impairments, I ever saw seemed to possess it. Later I was glad I did, after some few weeks of practice he was able to travel a bit further from our house. Without the need to crawl or kneel after few steps, the stick gave him a huge smile and a little freedom.

The little freedom of walking allowed him to go and look for friends further than our homestead. This is how he discovered the other use of the stick, assaulting his mates. Believe me when I say he wasn't a bully he only beat up those who used to laugh or mock him about his eyesight. I was proud of him, at first, but it later turned out that he was really a bully. Once or twice every other week, an adult from the village would come to complain to the pastor about his grandson's hitting their child. It became a norm that caused the grandfather to specifically ask me to take away the stick from Takura.

No, I told the grandfather, Takura needs the stick to walk and defend himself out there it's a cruel world for boys like him.

The pastor did not understand, he believed in holy love. He wanted Takura to take everything in because his rewards and blessings were heavenly. He tried to teach him about love and doing good to your neighbour, but it was already too late.

Takura and I used to stroll around the village together a lot that people started to believe he was my son. I encouraged them; I didn't find any fault in it. It didn't sound strange when he started calling me father, although for a while I had to explain repeatedly to my then girlfriends the existence of this motherless child. The sight of us walking hand in hand was so touching that some villagers offered us some coins. We took them, bought ourselves some sweets, we didn't need their pity, a little acknowledgement that Takura was like another child was enough.

He was like any other children, Takura was. In our happy hours I used to teach him to whistle and play a drum. He was way better at singing and dancing than me, I later learnt. He was afraid of water and I had to give up teaching him swimming because he couldn't let go off my hands when we were in the water. It wouldn't come as a surprise that ploughing and herding cattle wasn't easy for him but shearing nuts, packing, and storing maize was something the entire family left him to take care on his own.

My mother wanted me to teach him how to play music, that way when he was old enough, he would make noises and tunes in streets and buses to warranty handouts from strangers. If I had been holier then, I would have just prayed for a better future for him. My mother was kind enough to teach him to wash his own clothes, I do believe she did it so that she could not touch the filthy blind bastard's underwear. I don't even know if my father acknowledged his presence at his homestead. Tilda never asked about him and I am glad he never asked of his mother too, I want to believe that he saw in me an uncle worth be a father. A kind family he deserved.

It has been two years since I last saw the boy. My father, the dear old pastor, sold one of his prized cows to send Takura to the special school that caters for his needs. The school is in the city and I can't afford to visit him. I couldn't tell if it was out of love or the desire to get rid of the bastard that drove my father to do such a selfless act, but I am glad he did. Now I can hope that there is a future and place for him in the society we live in. Despite being in the same city with his mother they have never met or talked since he was six. We regularly send each other letters, although his have become less frequent than ever. He kind can't find a person kind enough to read and write his letters, Takura claims. It doesn't matter, I always tell him, you will always have a special place in my life.

This story first appeared in *When Hope lingers a little longer*

Dearest Monica

Two weeks after my daughter started attending a local community college in our neighbourhood, she woke up to find a woman staring into her eyes. She flew out of the bed, dashed downstairs, where the rest of the family was having breakfast, screaming that a ghost was trying to rip her soul out through her eyes. She screamed even more when she turned around to see the cloudy and unclear woman still hovering few inches in the air, right behind her. When she couldn't scream anymore, she collapsed on the floor and fainted.

I finished my bread and coffee and went to where she lay. Even unconscious, Emily looked small and innocent for a teenager with juvenile record and a history of drug abuse. Her dyed green hair didn't do any good to match her perfectly dark skin. She had always complained that she wasn't outstanding. She was wrong. In her usual shorts and bikini outfit I could swear she was not my daughter. I am sure the rest of the huge family thought so as I picked and placed her on the couch where she lay comfortably for some feel minutes.

My mother, who sat on the head of the table, stood up without touching her bread and came where I stood looking down at Emily. The face she wore, my mother, told of questions she was about to slap my daughter with. I knew most of those wouldn't be answered and the whole thing would end up being a sermon or a teaching my mother would deliver until lunch. She was the priestess after all. She was wearing her usual holy attire, a green plain dress with a matching head towel, jingles and beads hanging on her neck and wrists and her chocolate-brown face was decorated with red ugly lines and marks.

Behind the priestess, I could see my older brother and his wife standing up following her. That's what they do, they follow behind

69

mommy everywhere she goes. They obey her every command, no wonder they are my mother's favourites. Their oldest son, who is of Emily's age, stood from the table and started marching flamboyantly where we adults stood. My wife stopped him with a gaze before ordering him back to the table where the rest of my two children, three of my brother's kids and my uncles and aunties with their children sat with their eyes on their plates not sure what to do in during that awkward moment.

My wife was kind enough to bring a glass of water from the kitchen. She poured half of it on Emily's face. Emily jolted back to life with her mouth wide open, ready to lash out her scream again. We all placed our fingers on our mouths to stop her from screaming, luckily it worked.

"So, you are a woman now?" My mother was the first to break the ice.

"Who was it?"

I let my mother take care of the situation, she looked more capable than I was. She had done it so many times to members of our family that everyone had started calling her the priestess.

"Who was it?" My wife asked again.

Emily looked up to everyone's face, confusion pasted on her face.

"Gloria, will you keep quiet. Your daughter wakes up to find that she can see ghosts and you are more interested in knowing who took her virginity?" My mother said without taking a breath. It was something that couldn't be said out loud in every family. I was embarrassed, so I shrugged for the three of us.

She is not my mother, that's what Emily usual screams whenever anyone one calls her my wife's daughter. I think I heard her say so.

My wife had raised Emily since she was three after Emily's mother had lost her soul to a Monica.

I was delusional I am sure; Emily was still in shock and it seems impossible for her to utter a word in such circumstances.

The priestess sat beside Emily on the couch and held her hand. She knew how to calm beasts and Emily was a wounded one.

"Emily my dear, I want you to calm down." The priestess said to her granddaughter, "I want you to look behind you, slowly."

Emily did take a glance behind her and saw the ghost patiently observing the small crowd. The ghost gave her a courtesy smile and Emily lost her mind. She leapt into the air and tried to escape upsetting tables and the couch, leaving my mother on the floor and the rest of the furniture in disarray. It took everything we got, my brother and I, to pin her down. After a while she calmed, and she forcefully gulped down the rest of the water my wife still held in her hand.

"When a descendant of our lineage knew a man or a woman for the first time," my grandmother started again after she had picked herself up from the floor, "their eyes are opened to see our guiding angel, Monica."

Monica wasn't an angel, we all knew that, but we couldn't tell the young ones that she was a collection of ghosts of our departed ancestors guiding them into adulthood. On our first sexual intercourse, we gain essence from our partners that allows us to see how our futures were influenced. Monica was the form the essence took. She would always be there, hovering around quietly and giving silent guidance.

My mother did a better job explaining it to Emily again for the thousandth time. After a while, Emily calmed and was able to eye

Monica suspiciously without bolting away. Monica made her way to the table where the rest of the family smiled at her arrival. They loved and worshipped her; we all did. Thus, in return she fed our family gave use advice and made us prosper.

From the kitchen table I could see my brother's eldest son with his mouth open.

"Who took it?" I could make out the words from his mouth.

Emily raised her finger in response. It would be weird to talk about her first sex intercourse I guess, especially with the whole family gathered.

I looked at my wife gazing at the spot where Monica had been a minute earlier, she didn't know she wasn't no longer there. She always hoped to see Monica one day, even for a glimpse. That, unfortunately, wasn't a gift she was meant to receive.

This story first appeared on World of Myth Magazine issue 100 October 2021

The Walking Dad

You finally see him on a Thursday evening. He is walking alone as always. You reach into your pocket to grab your phone and take a photo of him to prove to your friends of his existence. Your pocket is empty, yes it means the phone is not there. You take a closer look at your pocket and discover a huge hole where the thief might have cut with a razor in order to steal your cellular phone. They actually call them smartphones these days and almost everyone has one, the man walking towards you definitely has one too. Or maybe not, he doesn't look like the usual dad who buys his wife and daughter an iPhone each whilst he is using an Android lollipop phone.

Who said anything about him being a dad? He might be a dad, you try to convince yourself. No, you correct yourself, he is just a father. A father is a man who produce offspring and a dad is a man who takes care of children: you mentally clap your hands for yourself, proud of your unquestionable wisdom. He might be a dad, he looks old and tired, all family men working and toiling for their loved ones do. His face is full of scars, you observe. From his face you assume he is in his late sixties.

"He is just fifty five." You recall Samson's words.

Yes Samson, you remember now, he is the one who took your phone because you couldn't pay him for his weed you took from his stash without his consent.

There is a huge reed hat on top of the man's head. It definitely came from Malawi, the weed not to the hat. You smoked the high quality stuff for the entire week without any side effects, well except that last time you thought you saw the dad carrying a satellite dish on his head instead of a simple weed hat-reed hat.

You believe that the price of clothes has doubled since they legalised marijuana that is why you are not surprised to see the walking figure clad in his birthday suit. Before you can cover your own eyes you see threads and shreds of rags that are covering the man's essentials. His pride as a father is hanging on a thread, literary. If anything was to happen to those tatters, would he be able to scrap it from the sand, you wonder. You are not sure what 'it' is. He doesn't care, you conclude, he is living in perpetual misery and walking around almost naked is not a big problem to him at all.

You pass each other at close proximity, too close you can say. He nods his head at you and you mumble a greeting in return.

"You stink old man!" You almost shout at the father as the smell of a body deprived bath for several week hit your nostrils hard, very hard. He is short and older, you have observed during the close encounter. He smells and his hands hang loosely on his shoulders. He walks with a slight and almost unnoticeable limp, you already knew that, he is missing few toes from his stint during the bush war. His feet are tiny and black with dirt, you couldn't have missed them since he is walking barefooted.

After you pass each other you stop and turn back. For a moment, just a tiny moment, you feel pity for him. You call his name, you know it, and it's also yours. He turns around and look at you with a deathly pale face.

"Loose change in your sock!" your mind screams at you. You take them out and count them. Seventy three cents. You throw it at his feet. He picks it up and shove it in what might have been a pocket if he was wearing real clothes. His thank you is almost like a whisper carried by a breeze. Before he turn his back on you to continue his journey to where no one knows, he looks at you one last time, his

74

white eyed blank face shows no sign of recognition or gratitude. You hate him for that but you continue staring at his back until he disappear out of your sight.

You turn and start making your way back to Samson's place. You start to think how you are going to tell your cousin that you gave his uncle some lose change to buy a half loaf of bread, that way he won't die yet to escape from his misery. You sit on the rock near the road and start to think if you should tell Samson that you waved your father goodbye for the last time, you hope not to see him ever again, just like he hoped when he abandoned you and your mother.

This was first published in Stripes Literary Magazine issue 2 volume 3 in October 2022

Home for Christmas

She had started talking to herself again, this time aloud and a lot. The first time was a couple of years back, when she was still sixty-seven. She had started earning few glances and awkward looks from strangers on the road whenever she was walking alone. She didn't know what was wrong until her favourite grandson, Bhiriyati, came to live with her and helped her regain her sanity. From that day she made everyone call her Mbuya Bhiriyati.

Mbuya Bhiriyati murmured under her breath as she limped towards the tarred road. The only tarred road on which buses from Harare travelled on. Soon, one of those buses would arrive and one of her children would disembark. Mbuya Bhiriyati didn't know which one of her children would be coming home for Christmas that year, she surely hoped it wasn't her youngest daughter Keresenzia.

Keresenzia had been the only child to visit her for three consecutive years. She always brought clothes and groceries with her and she had never stayed for Christmas to finish the food. She would be in a rush to get back to work, somewhere in Jo'burg. For those three times she had visited, she had made sure to leave an infant on Mbuya Bhiriyati's lap. Keresenzia was busy making babies across the borders with a man Mbuya Bhiriyati knew nothing about. Heck, she didn't know if all her three children had the same father! The thought of Keresenzia coming home for Christmas just to dump her newest child made Mbuya Bhiriyati want to spit.

She did spit under the Musasa tree. The tree, which stood tall and proud along the road, gave people waiting for the bus a shelter from the harsh rains and scorching sun. Not that Mbuya Bhiriyati needed protection from either, it was already late in the afternoon and the December sky didn't promise any rain.

It hadn't rained in a few days. The ground was dry and warm. Mbuya Bhiriyati liked to feel the sand on her feet, it was the reason she usually walked barefooted. She was barefooted on that Friday evening. She wore a black long dress, the one she used to work with in the fields. She was wrapped around a brown floral Zambia and its matching doek. Mai Jemusi had brought them for her on her last visit.

Mai Jemusi's last visit had been five years ago. Five years, that was how long Mbuya Bhiriyati had last seen her eldest daughter. Her daughter had walked out after Mbuya Bhiriyati had asked her when her husband was going to pay the bride price. Mai Jemusi had eloped with a man when she was still a teenager in school. That was twenty years ago. The man might have simply forgotten that he still owed the bride price to his in-laws. After that encounter where Mbuya Bhiriyati reminded her daughter of that commitment, she never set foot in her hut again. Mbuya Bhiriyati had made sure to pray for her oldest daughter every night.

The night was upon her when the last bus from Harare stopped under the Musasa tree. It had been a while, Mbuya Bhiriyati had decided to sit in the muddy mud to rest of her feet. The bus was packed. It was Christmas after all and people were traveling home to their families, would her family be coming home too? She wondered. She stared at each passenger as they disembarked, waiting hoping to recognise something familiar.

A familiar figure, broad shouldered and tall made its way out of the bus. A sigh of relief escaped from Mbuya Bhiriyati's mouth. At least one of her children had come home for Christmas. Mbuya Bhiriyati stood up and made her way to her son who seemed oblivion of her presence. He looked distracted and in search of something. His luggage of course, he found it and stood a moment chatting with fellow passengers. Mbuya Bhiriyati came and hugged her son him from behind. She could feel him tense his muscles in her tight hug. Then her son turned around.

"I am sorry, my son, I thought you were someone else," she stammered an apology.

The stammering was all an act. She wasn't sorry for hugging the stranger at all. She had missed the touch of her son. Even as she had seen the man disembark from the bus, she had known it wasn't her son. Her son wasn't coming home for Christmas that year. He hadn't come the previous year and he wouldn't be coming ever again. The government had taken him away from her.

The government had sent him to a foreign country to fight in a war for diamonds. Democratic Republic of Congo, that's where her only son had disappeared in. A letter from the government had told her that her son wasn't dead, just missing in action. She had waited for two years and hadn't received any news about her son's whereabouts. Except once when they told her about compensation. She thought they were going to give her the diamonds her son fought for. No, it was just some few dollars and she never received a cent of it. Her daughter in-law grabbed it all and ran away with her boyfriend. That cheating whore had been a headache to Mbuya Bhiriyati and she was glad to see her gone. What Mbuya Bhiriyati was grateful for was that, the whore had left Bhiriyati behind.

Bhiriyati was a sweet young boy of thirteen. He had his father's name, the one who went missing in a war, who also had his father's name, the one Mbuya Bhiriyati had married years earlier. Years which she thought she was happy.

"When I think of happiness," Bhiriyati the husband had said," I think of you and me waiting at a bus stop for our children to bring their spouses and children for Christmas."

Every Christmas Eve Mbuya Bhiriyati had made sure to wait for her children and grandchildren at the bus stop. Just to keep her husband's dream alive. Mbuya Bhiriyati had never married again after her husband had died during the war. Bhiriyati the husband had died during the war, Bhiriyati the son had gone missing in a raging war what would also happen to Bhiriyati the grandson? Mbuya Bhiriyati brushed away the thought of a curse running in the family.

She was running late. The bus had already drove off. The people who had disembarked had carried their bags and walked into the night. Even the son man whom she had given a hug had gone, not before throwing a weird look in her direction. She was now all alone, in a world of seven billion people. She stood up, looked up to the stars in prayed prayer and slowly made her way back to her homestead where Bhiriyati and the other grandchildren waited for their Christmas Eve supper.

"Maybe they will come next Christmas," She muttered to herself, not sure how much hope was in the lie that had come out of her mouth

Coming Home

Every second Friday of each month, I always make sure to call folks at home. My mother usually answers. She misses me and would love to see me again. I miss her too and I would love to be her young son again.

"When are you coming back home Takesure, my son?" She whimpers on the other end of the receiver, "I am now old, do you want me to die without setting my eyes on my own son again?"

"I will be home for Christmas, I promise." I continue, "I have to go and work mom, have a wonderful day."

I drop the call before she can call on my lie. This is the third Christmas I have promised to be home; we both know it's a lie. I am no longer ashamed of lying to her, I lie to myself all the time.

I slum myself back onto the bed. I am in a one roomed cottage I rent behind a hair salon. This room contains everything I own in this goddamn country; two blankets, 3 pairs of trousers, four shirts, two socks of assorted colours, one pair of shoes, two pots, and a fork. Everything that I have bought for the past 3 years. Neither a plate nor a stove is in sight. I don't own the bed; it was there when I moved in.

I make myself comfortable on the bed. I don't have to work, I lied, I have been unemployed for the last two years. At the last place I worked, I was let go for misplacing company property. It was a construction firm, the only one in Polokwane to hire foreigners. I was fortunate that they didn't involve the police. Otherwise I would have been deported after serving a jail time for stealing and selling their shovels. It would probably been worse since I do not have proper documentation to be in the country.

It's a Saturday evening and I am laying on my bed listening to the sound of traffic outside my room. I can't peek outside to see what's happening. The room doesn't have any windows, it used to be a storeroom. It's always dark and the air stinks. I miss the sound of singing birds, the fresh smell of trees and flowers and the warmth of the Zimbabwean sun. Sure, the sun here is merciless and unforgiving.

I clean myself and put on some clean clothes. It's now pretty dark outside and it's time to make money. I go outside and knock on the hair salon's back door. The landlady's daughter opens the door. There is a sly smile on her face as I greet her. She goes back into the salon after mumbling what I assume to be a reply. She comes back few moments later with a crate of boiled eggs wrapped around with a plastic. She hands them to me with her eyes on the ground, embarrassed to make eye contact. She is a couple of years younger than me. I pull myself together, she is still in high school and the landlady would have me beaten to death or something worse if she finds out that I laid my hand on her daughter. I thank the girl and disappear into the night.

"Mae! Mae! Mae!" I am at the bus terminal, screaming eggs at the passengers through the bus windows. Most of them politely look away but same threaten to call the rank marshals and have me escorted away. I move away from those passengers. I prefer the drunk, they always buy an egg or two to consume with hot chilli sauce.

One drunk customer, a regular at the terminal, sits at the bench glaring in my direction. I walk up to him and offer him an egg with an option of paying the following day. He shakes his head and dozes off. I move on to another passengers.

"Makwere-makwere go back to your own country!" The drunk suddenly ejaculates into the night and a blanket of silence engulfs the whole terminal.

Makwere-makwere, that's what the South Africans call us all the foreigners in their country. They say it's the way we foreigners walk without raising our feet from the ground that they, the South Africans, are able to identify us as foreigners. Every time someone call me that, I feel like peeling my face skin and running stoke naked in the city centre. They hate us here. I hate it here. I wish I were home, but I can't.

The silence continues deafening, drowning out the sound of the bus engines. All eyes are on me. I walk away, with my head barely that high. There is a paid toilet at the terminal, I rush to hide behind it. Despite the shame burning on my face, I know I can't afford to pay to cry in peace. I pretend to sleep for half an hour or so.

It's almost ten pm when I show myself at the terminal again. Except for a couple of buses half-filled, the terminal is almost devoid of people. Most of my fellow vendors have retired for the night. Some women are hurdling together on a corner. They speak my native language and are from my country. I pretend not to see them. They might feel uncomfortable selling their bodies if they know I am watching. I know most of them. One has a husband and a son, boarding near the hair salon I live behind. The other one is saving up to send her daughter to college. I can't judge, it is what it is.

The last bus leave and I start preparing to hit a couple of night clubs to sell my boiled eggs. Almost a dozen eggs remain and fortunately they are still lurking warm to attract some customers.

"Police!" Someone shouts and we all scatter into the night.

I run blindly, not knowing where I will find safety. I trip and fall. I pick myself up and leave the eggs on the ground; the police can't catch me. I know what they will do to be. They will deport me to Zimbabwe. I can't go back home. No, not just yet.

This story was first published in The Queensdale Report issue 85 in February 2023

The Little Switch

You are clad in a protective silver jumpsuit and the orange helmet is in your left hand. You walk slowly to the middle of the workshop where the tin is waiting for you. You trip upon some metals and tools, curse, and lie to yourself that one day you will clean the shop and give the business back its sanity and back to glory. The workshop is a huge hall with some dimmed lights far up on the ceiling.

Your brother walks behind you with some papers. He is older and slower, but he is still the smartest being alive, he built the tin after all. He is just six years older than you, but age has taken a huge visible toil on his frail body. It is understandable, he has never slept for the past fifty years or so building the tin.

Of course, there's the tin. You run your fingers on the white box, it is metallic cold. You wonder why they don't call it the toilet, everything about it reminds you of the stalls in the public toilets. You walk around it, impressed by its tiny size and functionality. It is small enough to allow only one individual to sit comfortably in and it is technologically advanced enough to send that individual to one specific day in the past, May the tenth 2025.

Your brother shoves you into the tin, forces the orange helmet over your head roughly and clip it shut. You willingly comply as he straps you on the seat. It's for your safety and the ride won't be a smooth one. Your brother reminds you of the mission, you do not listen though you have heard it a million times before. He tells you to pull the switch only when he gives the signal. He closes the glass hatch and runs to the other side of the workshop where the rest of the controls and the tech guys are.

You wait patiently for the signal. Sweat start oozing from your forehead. Either it's getting hot in the tin or you are just nervous. There isn't any air-conditioning in the tin to prove the former and unfortunately there is nothing you can do about it now; your fate has already been sealed. There is only one small switch on this entire machine, nothing else. You start gentle caressing it, taking great pains not to flip it since your entire family's life depend upon it. You know you are supposed not to flip the switch; you are not going to flip the switch but then your hand flips the switch anyway.

You are confused. You look up from the hatch and see your brother smiling. He raises his hand and waves at you. You try to wave or shout back but you cannot move. You scream in silence to abort. Every single cell in your body is screaming in pain. This is not supposed to be happening. Then an orange light devours you in a flash.

You are sitting on the banks of Zambezi River alone and you feel weird wearing a helmet and a protective suit. You can move your body again, thank God, and the pain is gone. You stand up and look around; the river is wider and there is garbage dumped around. You remember the scene from when you were still a child. The tin must have done its magic, you shout in amazement. Downstream you notice three little children swimming. The oldest is a boy, probably ten. There is also a girl almost of the same age or she might be younger, you are not sure. You don't bother with the toddler of four, it looks harmless. The oldest one, the boy, croaks with joy, jumping and dancing in the shallow water. He splashes water on himself and let the sun glitter on the droplets stuck on his dark skin. You are embarrassed to look at the naked girl to see if she is enjoying herself also. Since the air is clean and there is nothing else to do you decide to watch the children to pass the time. The toddler then decides to go to relieve itself behind the bushes, the oldest one, the boy, runs after it ordering it back with immediate effect.

The girl is left alone sitting at edge of the river. Damn it! You remember the mission now; save the girl from drowning! You start to run along the river like a lunatic, gasping for air, like a dying horse, in your helmet. You almost reach the little brown skinned girl, twenty meters away maybe, then she sees you tumbling downstream. She is startled by you; she backtracks and falls with a thud into the water. She can't swim, no one has ever taught her to. You reach where she was a second earlier and you believe there is nothing you can do. The current is too strong, and you are terrified to jump after her. Before you kneel to cry, a silver light sucks you whole from the above.

You look up from the hatch and see your brother smiling. You are confused. This is not supposed to happen, you know it. He raises his hand and waves at you. You try to wave or shout, but your body is paralyzed. Nothing comes out when you try to shout to him to stop, your body cannot take this kind of pain, it's like you are dipped in acid. Then the orange light devours you again.

There is a river in front of you, you recognize it, it's the Zambezi River. You know what is to be done so you search for the three children. They are upstream. You see the younger version of yourself running to defecate behind the bushes. Your older brother, the smartest being alive, barks after you to come back. He is in charge after all. He follows you to where you are squatting but you are four and can only leave when you think you are done.

Your sister continues bathing in the cool waters of the great river. She lets the water run from hair short black hair, through her skin to her tiny feet. Once or twice she dips her legs into the water. She can't swim, you remember that now, so she wouldn't do anything riskier than that.

Whatever you are seeing you know it will only end with your sister drowning. She has already drowned once but you are there to stop it. You are smart, you tell yourself, so you won't run upstream to grab her before the calamity, she might get startled and end up falling in the river. You don't know how you come up with that but it a sound logical in your head. So, you wait and hope for a miracle.

Nothing out of ordinary happens. The sister calls to the old brother to hurry. She looks in their direction before she jumps. You try not to believe it, but your eyes have already seen it. This is how it happened when you were still kids? Everyone blamed your brother and he vowed not to sleep until he made it right.

The current so strong that your sister reaches downstream where you are few seconds later. You loved her, you do love her and it's only natural that you jump into the river to save her. You grab her leg and pull the both of you out of the river. You were never the one afraid of water. Both of you are still coughing and vomiting gallons of water when silver light hits your eyes and suck you through voids of the unknown.

The pain is excruciating when you open your eyes. Your brother is smiling whilst looking down the hatch. You scream to abort, but it's all in your head. Your body is paralyzed so you cannot wave or do anything but that doesn't stop your brother from raising his hand and wave at you. Then the orange lights blind you for the millionth time. You are confused but you know well that this isn't supposed to be happening

Blue

Earth is a terrible place to live. So, I have been told. It is crowded and dirty. Water is scarce and the air is polluted. Wars and crimes are rampage. It's the only planet where reproduction restrictions are still enforced.

"You should be grateful that you were born on The Hub." An oldie always says after telling us about the woes of the planet our ancestors once called home.

I am grateful for being born and raised on The Hub. I am grateful for calling it home, this crappy piece of metal orbiting around the planet q3 in Proxima Centaury is my home. I am grateful for the oldies that guide us and give us the wisdom and the expertise needed to colonise the planet beneath us.

"The planet beneath us is a fertile rock waiting for our taking," Baba Mafeso says every day. He is one of the three oldies left. At a century and half Earth years old the man is still as healthy as a swine. He grew up on Earth, playing near the ocean before volunteering to join the exploratory ship to Proxima centaur q3. The journey took almost 120 years of his life, yet he says he regrets nothing.

"Today we will be exploring the northern pole of this planet," the elderly pauses for a minute, "and I will be taking with me only three cadets."

We are in the engineering room, hastily preparing the landing shuttle for the yet to be named descending crew. Three cadets, I can be one of them, I shoot my hand up with eleven others.

"No, I don't want volunteers." Baba Mafeso says," I will choose whom I will go down with."

This is the third visit to the planet, and it makes sense that Baba Mafeso chooses the best and the most capable of his team. Three seats, twelve cadets of varying ages and belonging to multiple genders. I am twenty and the oldest, I think I deserve the seat. The officer's brown eyes stare at each one of us in the room. Wrinkles form on his dark forehead as he thinks why each of us deserve not to go.

Mafeso is the darkest skinned man I have ever seen. He keeps his head bald and is always well shaven as per his job's requirements, he is the Chief Officer, same as being the Captain. Every day he wears his old blue uniform, the one the guerillas wore when they fought in the war for the restoration of our ancestral planet. He was on the losing side.

"When I was a boy, my grandfather used to tell me how he used to play with sand on the beach, it was the purest joy a boy could have." Mafeso once told us, "However my father told me a different story, when he was young, he didn't play on the beach, it was one of the dirtiest places in the region. The ocean water had now been filled with plastics, dead fish and nuclear waste. By the time I was born the Port of Beira which my family had called home for hundreds of years was no more, covered with water which continued to rise from the ocean."

Mafeso's family resettled in the inland, it was there he met my grandparents and others who also believed something could be done for the future. *For the future*, those three words were written everywhere on The Hub. The oldies always say it's to remind us the reason we left Earth.

"Ncube, Munotyei and Joshua." Mafeso's voice jolts me back to the engineering room, "Get your gear ready and meet me here in an hour for the drop."

89

****

When I think of happiness, I imagine myself walking barefoot on the sand. I imagine holding my sister's hand whilst gazing upon the ocean. I imagine her face dazzling with a smile and her mouth singing songs of joy. I have always looked forward to the day I would find happiness on this planet in Proxima centaur.

What I did not expect was ice, acres of it. Frozen blocks of water as far as the eye could see. I can't stop myself imagining the cold taking hold of my leg and I having to break it off to save my life. I don't need to worry about though, I am wearing bodysuit and it protects every inch of my body.

"We should go the long way," Munotyei screams on the intercom, her voice louder than necessary, "there is a glacier up ahead."

The Chief Officer's voice calmly tells me to follow Munotyei. Munotyei is as ace, a perfect student that outshines in everything. Between her and me, it perfectly makes sense that I carry the heavy equipment whilst she and Mafeso led the way with the fancy tiny computers. Joshua had been ordered to stay with the landing shuttle.

"Ncube please try to keep up." Mafeso barks.

"Yes sir!" I howl back and continue trotting in the barren ice land. With every step I take my foot sink in few inches of condensed water only for me to take it out and sink it somewhere else. Whatever I am going through I know it is not as better as what my sister is going through. She is in the infirmary on The Hub, hooked to the machines that keep her alive.

"Under the cliff there," her voice comes again over the intercom, "it's the perfect spot to set up the equipment."

I drag the huge box in the direction she is pointing. There is no need to confirm with the Officer, he always agrees with her. A hundred of yards away I can see why she chose the place; one can appreciate the ugliness and the barrenness of the hopeful planet without freezing to death. A small cave protects the admirer from the raging ice winds.

I am not an admirer, no. I am an explorer preparing for the human colonisation of the planet. The Hub is the first human interstellar ship to visit this solar system, by my rudimentary calculations I am the tenth or eleventh human to set foot on the planet Hope. I feel pride seeping in my suit as I watch Munotyei and Mafeso set up the equipment and machines I help carry.

Those damn machines, they are connected to the hub, the same way my sister is connected to it. She cannot be separated from it without losing her life. She has got the disease of the stomach; hundreds of children lose their lives to the disease every cycle. They bleed in the stomach and die. No one says it out loud but everyone knows it's the food. Recycled nutrients from waste and deceased Hub residents, mixed with plastics then 3D printed and served on a silver platter is the only food we have known our whole lives.

If the planet is as futile as they had taught us on The Hub, we will start seeding and finally have real food. I look around as I see ice as far the horizon, hope is not what I feel.

****

The icy wind continues raging. I check my suit; the temperature is way below negative 200 degrees Celsius. This place is hostile to the human species.

"Cadets! Where's is that beeping coming from?" Baba Mafeso asks.

"It's from the atmospheric gauge. It is reading trace amounts of nuclear waste."

I look around for a spot to rest. From the heaps of ice under the cliff I dig small hole and crawl in, I can't be caught naked in this wind.

"Where is it coming from?"

"I don't know, maybe from the grounds or fissures," Munotyei doesn't know where to point, "You understand we are talking about traces amounts, not enough to do harm right?"

"From a damaged battery maybe?" They stare at me as I lift a canister up for them to see. "And It's not my battery, don't be horrified please, I found it on ice when I sat down."

It is the same make and model of nuclear-powered battery that each of us have in our suits. The batteries are the main source of power outside The Hub. It does look peculiar to see one laying around, even if it was damaged.

"Where did you get it?" Baba Mafeso asks and it seems he doesn't understand what it happening. I tell him again where I had found it.

Baba Mafeso leaps from the fancy computers and start digging with his hands where my buttocks had been a minute earlier. He keeps on mumbling, asking no one in particular where the battery has come from. Munotyei and I share a knowing look. Extended duration in space has been linked to madness, it is an unproven hypothesis though.

We stand few paces away from the maniac digging in the ice. None of us sure what to do. His hands suddenly hit something, he meticulous clears the ice to reveal a bodysuit helmet, identical to us. The glass is shattered and I can see the human skull clearly.

"No, it can't be." One of us says out loud, I don't know who.

Baba Mafeso tries to pull the helmet and its occupant from the sand. He ends up pulling out the half of the suit. It's orange, none of the suits on The Hub are orange. I try to release a sigh of relief. The suit is old, it had probably been here on the planet years before The Hub had arrived. The dead explorer isn't one of us. Despite the suit being old and torn almost to bits, the three words on the left breast are as clear as light, *For the Future.*

For the future; three simple words that had propelled us decades into the future, millions of miles from our specie's home. Three simple words we now see on a dead past, a rugged history of bones and hopelessness. Three simple words which meant more in this moment but worth nothing after that.

This story first appeared The World of Myth Magazine Issue 115 in January 2023

Mourning and Sunset

Evening was already upon him as he made his way towards the village. He hadn't realised how time had glided past him; one moment the sun was mercilessly scalding his forehead and the next it was orange in colour snuggling comfortably into its mother's bosom. Tapera had walked the entire day and still had a long journey ahead of him before he could reach the village. The rumbling of his stomach reminded him that he had not eaten anything since the previous evening. Neither had a drop of water touched his lips. The tattered clothes he wore were now slowing his tired body down.

The events of the previous evening weighed heavily on his mind. Death and gore were all it had been all about. He still didn't believe that overnight his well-planned life and brightly lit future had crumbled down to dust. It was something Tapera had never imagined would ever happen to him. He had been on the verge of success. He would have been the richest man in the seven villages. They actually; they would have been the richest men in town, Tapera and Phiri.

The rumbling of the stomach came again, it wasn't hunger it was diarrhoea! Tapera quickly turned out of the well-trodden path and hid himself in the bushes. A sigh of relief escaped his mouth as he sprayed and drowned an entire colony of ants with his insides. Nothing was ever going to grow on that place again.

"Good evening to you."

A young woman, possibly not older than him, was passing through the road and greeted him. Tapera mumbled a reply. The woman continued her way but not before Tapera had noticed a thick layer of petroleum jelly pasted on her dark skin. The yellow dress she wore wasn't easy to miss and Tapera would have avoid such an embarrassment if he had looked careful enough before he has squatted and defecated beside the road.

In a minute or so Tapera was back on the road. He did not have enough time to dwell on his embarrassment, he had news of death to deliver. News of Phiri's death. Phiri had been a friend who turned brother and Tapera knew the news of his death had to reach Phiri's parents from him, not from strangers or the police. Phiri's family deserved to receive it from someone they knew.

Until this fateful day Tapera had always assumed that he could walk the thirty-five-kilometre trek between Pote River and Musana village in half a day. He had even tried to make a bet with Phiri a couple of weeks back when they left for the river, to mine gold. Gold-panners, that was what the government and other fancy people called them but the duo and the other hundreds of people digging in the pits didn't mind if they were called makorokoza. That's what they did, dig small pits along the river and pan tiny amounts of gold with mercury in a dish and sell to a buyer with ready cash. It wasn't legal but it brought the food on the table. It was the kind of job that made no one strong enough to walk long distances. Tapera thought so as he dragged his feet towards the reminder of the journey.

What Tapera could have killed for, as he walked, was a pint of cold beer. Cold opaque beer like the one they bought when they came up from the pits. Some women sold it to them, expensive but worth every cent.

"So, you are drinking beer now?" Tapera's mother had asked when he had first come back home from work. He didn't find the need to explain himself, now that he was a man. If he earned the money, he had the right to buy whatever he wanted with it, even beer despite him being just seventeen. The boys he worked with, way younger than him, drank alcohol everyday like addicts and it was normal. Tapera tried to tell his family that but they didn't understand. They thought alcohol would be the death of him and Phiri. Alcohol hadn't been the death of Phiri, it was a bottle of water that led to his death.

Tapera reached the Supa growth point. It was heft with activity as expected of a Thursday evening. The seven dilapidated buildings served the community well despite three of them being bars and beer halls. The rest of the buildings served as grocery stores and a grain-miller. Tapera had grew up playing at the area, he knew every inch of the place. He also knew every person who happened to be selling their wares along the road. The regulars at the beer hall greeted him loudly. He could tell the news of the previous night had reached them and they were pretending to be oblivious so he could tell them the hot gossip. Tapera passed them with his head over his shoulders.

Chigwedere Sports bar stood with its inviting doors wide open. He would have been a fool not to accept its invitation. One too many times, Tapera had accompanied Phiri inside the building to drag out Phiri's intoxicated father and haul him home to his wife. Phiri's father was the benchmark of all the drunkards in the village, no one adored slavery to the ancient liquid than him. Most of the year, Phiri's father lay in a pool of his own vomit inside the beer hall and now the task had fallen upon Tapera to lift the old man up now, drag him to his mourning wife.

A sigh of relief, loud enough to drown the loud music in the beer hall, escaped from Tapera's mouth as he entered the hall. Phiri's father wasn't amongst the horde of men who sat drowning their sorrows with alcohol, he was nowhere to be seem inside the beer hall. Tapera walked over to the counter, threw a couple of bills to the bartender, and pointed to a scud of beer. The bartender did not bother to check the minor's ID. The bartender with the money in hand gladly parted with the bottle of beer. The boy, with the beer in hand, went and sat on an empty bench. The loud music was just a whisper to the silence of his soul.

He took the first sip. It was in memory of Phiri who had been murdered with a shovel by a fellow panner. Phiri had taken a sip from the mukorokoza's water bottle without permission and the mukorokoza had retaliated with violence. He gulped half of the remaining contents of the beer. Tapera hadn't seen any of it, he had been busy looking for one of his shoelaces. Few seconds later he was at the door, with the holy blood coursing through his veins, determined to pass on the news of his friend's death.

The girl with the yellow dress stood at the door, hesitating to enter the hall. Tapera greeted the familiar face with a wide grin on his face. The girl politely answered with a sly smile on her face. No, she wasn't a girl, she looked old enough to be Tapera's mother. She offered her services to the boy.

The boy looked out into the night, little stars were already dancing in the sky. It wouldn't do any good to bring news of death before supper. Maybe he could wait a bit whilst he rested and convince the woman in the yellow dress that he didn't need her services. Surely Phiri could wait a bit, Tapera was already in mourning.

This story was first published in Zimbolicious Anthology volume 6 in 2021

Insignificant Dot

It's a dark night, you can't tell weather the clouds are dispersing yet, but the splattering on your face tells you the rain isn't receding. You stumble and trip on an uneven ground. You recover your balance by stepping into a puddle of water. You don't feel the cold or the weight of your wet clothes - it's because you are a ghost. Not an actual spirit of the dead hovering around in the air but you feel like a ghost. This is because you are dead on the inside and you feel stuck - unable to move on with life - the same way the departed souls are chained down in the limbo. A breathing ghost caught in the purgatory called life that is exactly what you are.

There you are, a living ghost, walking in the rain on a January evening. The abandoned streets of Kambuzuma mirroring the loneliness in you. The partially lit streetlights reflecting the darkness that makes you. You don't need the streetlights nor other pedestrians, you know the way very well. You have been taking the same route for the past few weeks, today is the last time you are going to be taking this nightly walk towards the river bank.

A flash of lighting - trees, wet grass and shacks and shanties where poverty lives. A crack of thunder - roaring water raging down in the river and rain droplets hitting the leaves and the hard ground. Inhaling burning suppers being cooked in the homes and the stinking human waste preserved behind those plastic and iron sheet dwellings. Cold air hugging your body. Raindrops caressing your forehead and all the way past your nose into your mouth. You tongue wiggle in contact with the particles from the cloud yet repulsed by the sourness of climate change.

For a brief moment, a millisecond maybe, you give in to your five senses and you feel alive again, you can start feeling the dead part of your self-resurrecting and starting to live again. The illusion of being a regular normal person gets shattered by one of the voices inside your head, "The dead in purgatory are better than you."

You know why they are better than you. They, the dead in the purgatory, are always feeling the constant longing to attain something that is beyond their reach whilst you, you feel nothing. You are hollow. The emptiness in you cancelling out the human nature that used to be you.

You ignore it, the voice in your head, and continue walking in the dark, away from the illegal dwellings, towards the river. That's where you and they, the dozen or so voices in your head, are finally going to come to terms with the situation. You know what they will tell you to do when you reach the river. That is why you brought the rope on your shoulders.

You reach the river. You start looking for the perfect tree branch to tie it up. You find the branch but not the rope. You did not bring the rope with you, actually you don't even own a rope. The one you had seen on your shoulders doesn't exist. You mind is playing tricks on you. You are lost in your thoughts again. You are not where you are supposed to be. You don't belong here, you don't belong anywhere else either. That makes you insignificant, like a dot.

You make up your mind to follow the river upstream. There is a bridge there and you can follow the road back home. As soon as you arrive home you have to talk to someone. You need help. You continue walking in the rain, towards the bridge, muttering to yourself what a failure you are.

You sigh as the voices in your head starts blabbering about your inadequacies. They list them and they are numerous. They weigh on you, like the wet clothes you are wearing. The failures and the inadequacies slow you down until you are trudging along the river. You fail to make yourself not to feel like a failure. Ah, the irony.

There you are, walking in the rain, the night dark and wet, your feet stiff, hard and slow on your way to a tomorrow you can't imagine. Maybe you will come back again the following week and try again, you are not sure of anything but what you are certain is that in this vast world you are so small and insignificant like a spark of dust. An Insignificant dot.

Uneven Sky

Uncle Bonnie walked slowly, like how all old men do, towards the huge tree on the Headman's homestead. His walking stick made a rattling sound as it hit the hard stones and pebbles on the gravel road. He kept on muttering how important he was and he could not be rushed by anyone, not even the village's top man. He did not care for the eyes of his fellow villagers as he approached the court of Headman Chirandu.

"Uncle Bonnie, I am glad you have managed to make time from your very busy and tight schedule to attend this mandatory court." The Headman said. There was a murmur of disapproval from the villagers who thought the headman's exaggerated welcome was inappropriate.

Uncle Bonnie sat on the ground away from his fellow villagers. The shade of the Msasa tree was a relief to the November sun. The tree provided enough shade to the villagers whenever they happened to need it, that is during political rallies and embarrassing justices dispersed by Chirandu.

Uncle Bonnie cursed and spat as he realised that he had sat on fresh cow dung. He moved to the other side of the tree where he sat on a small patch of grass, away from the comfort of the tree's shadow and at the mercy of the scorching midday sun.

Chirandu cleared his throat and bellowed out, "Lets proceed."

A man stood up. He looked sixty, almost Uncle Bonnie's age. He politely took off his reed hat. The man was wearing a worn out shirt, which might have been white in its former glory, and an old brown pair of trousers which was now in tatters. Uncle Bonnie cursed and spat again as he realised that the man was Baba Tindo, his neighbour, who always found a way to quarrel with him every other week.

Baba Tindo clapped his hand and made a disgusting sound as he cleared his throat to address the assembly.

"Headman Chirandu, I salute you. What brought me here is the issue of my maize field." He stopped as he looked around to see if anyone was listening.

The pause made the impatient Chief to bark at him angrily, "What about it?"

"Well, last week Uncle Bonnie's youngest grandson deliberately started a fire which burnt the surrounding perimeter of my maize field." said Baba Tindo.

There was a murmur among the villagers; some felt sympathy for the old man, some thought that their time was being wasted and some were thrilled by the man's lose.

"Not only that, some people decided to herd their cattle into my vulnerable field. The cows, I learnt afterwards, were Uncle Bonnie's. It was also his granddaughter who let in the cows." The man continued.

He is a great actor, thought Uncle Bonnie. There was an eruption of noise from the angry mob who demanded instant justices. Uncle Bonnie sat silently, amused. Some of his so called friends were already demanding him to pay two cows to his neighbour and a goat to the court.

Baba Tindo, however, did not sit down. He raised his right hand to quieten the crowd and continued to narrate his misfortunes. "Not only that my good people, Uncle Bonnie's youngest son impregnated my daughter and he is now refusing responsibility."

The raging crowd grew quiet and looked at Uncle Bonnie who felt like he didn't belong anywhere else but hell. The uncomfortable stares made him play with the hem of his shirt. His posture and silence made the court to take it as a guilty plea. Only Chirandu, amongst the multitude present, was the only one who was not ecstatic about the allegations. He had already helped Uncle Bonnie to evade prosecution twice. However, this time he would not or else tongues would start wiggling. If he wanted to retain the villagers' loyalty he had to deal with Uncle Bonnie accordingly. This was a responsibility he hated much.

"What have you to say for yourself Uncle Bonnie?" Headman Chirandu asked.

The man looked startled at the mentioning of his name and looked confused for a second. He removed his new and expensive leather hat, clapped his hands and stood up looking straight into the Chief's eye.

"This is outrageous!" screamed Uncle Bonnie. "This whole matter is trivia!"

The angry man looked around to weigh his words on the shocked faces. The words had the desired effect. He continued, "If you don't want me in this poor village of yours, I will leave!"

"My grandson John went to the city two weeks ago and I don't know how he burnt your fence from there Baba Tindo. Why don't you ask your sons they are the ones who smoke stolen cigarettes in that field, maybe they left a burning stub?" Uncle Bonnie said looking at Baba Tindo who sat uncomfortable in the crowd.

"My granddaughter was admitted at the hospital a fortnight ago with bilharzia and you tell me she drove my cattle into your maize field? No, this is ridiculous!"

"Did anyone tell you that your daughter was caught again with another herd boy from the Maude villager? Don't look surprised Baba Tindo everyone knows it, it's a shame you don't know what your girl is up to. Then you claim it was my son who impregnated her? My son was still in university that time."

The man looked around was satisfied by what he saw, his fellow villagers hadn't expected any theatricals.

"Headman Chirandu," Uncle Bonnie turned to direct his words to Chirandu, "I own a huge herd of cattle, and I am not offering any to Baba Tindo. I can't reward him for being a bad neighbour. Neither am I giving this court a single one but I will be giving them all to the mission hospital in Maude village."

"You are giving away all of your cattle?" asked one of the few concerned villager.

"I won't be in need of them in the city." said Uncle Bonnie smiling again.

"You are going to the City?" asked the Headman.

"Yes, I am relocating with my family to the city."

"What about your school?" asked the concerned villager.

"It had been providing free education to your children for years now but now it's time to stop that nonsense. I am shutting down my store too. No more free medicine and groceries for you from my shop, I am moving it to the city. My truck, which I used to ferry you and your tomatoes to the city market, will be loaded with my grain. The grain I have been sharing with you these lean years then I will be gone."

Uncle Bonnie bowed and walked away slowly from the court leaving the stunned villagers to their thoughts. There was smirk on his face. He knew the village needed him. There was no future without him. Soon the villagers would come to beg him to stay. The villagers would do anything to keep him. They, Uncle Bonnie knew, would rather banish the innocent Baba Tindo from the village in order for the devil with the gifts to stay with them.

The Voicemail

Despite growing up on a farm in Mozambique I never learnt to wake up early in the morning. It was of great annoyance when my phone rang up way before five o'clock. I answered half asleep.

"What the hell, Raina?" Suzie's voice came from the other end of the phone, "What do you mean you are sneaking out of the country?"

"What are you talking about Suzie?" I was trying to be polite. We haven't spoken to each other in months, since the incident.

"For God's sake if you have sold my laptop already I will hunt you down wherever you think are safe." Suzie's threats were back again.

I switched on the bed lamp, glanced at the cabinet where she had left her laptop months earlier and found it sitting comfortably and gathering dust.

"Don't go crazy on me bitch." I tried to sound tough, it wasn't my style, "I am not the one who cursed you."

"You sent me a voicemail late last night saying you were selling my laptop in order to get money to get out of the country. You promised to pay me back. You said something about someone impersonating you and the police chasing after you for a crime you didn't commit. Am I wrong?" Suzie's voice was now a bit calmer.

"Yes, you are wrong," I answered, "I never said such thing. You laptop is still here and you can come and take it anytime."

I dropped the call before she could respond. I didn't want to give her the laptop back and I knew there was no way she would show her face to my home ever again. She had brought it on our last sleepover. The following morning she left her laptop behind but took my husband with her. That was about six months earlier and I had never seen them since.

It was still pretty dark outside, I decided to sleep another hour before I could start getting ready for work. I only managed to get myself depressed for an hour, thinking how my best friend of 14 years had taken my husband away from me.

***

I ended up being late to work. It was almost eight when I arrived. I went straight to Theo's office to apologise. He would understand. That man had been nothing but a saint since day one.

"Raina how are you?" Theo said upon my entrance in his office.

"I good sir, how are you?" I continued, "sorry sir I am late again."

He motioned me to sit on a chair. His office wasn't that lavishly furnished; we sold plastic chairs in Thouyandou after all and it wasn't much of a big business. He seemed to have aged like a decade in the couple of days. He was under a lot of stress; someone had embezzled almost 10 thousand rand from his business. I assumed that was what he wanted to talk about, hopefully he had found the culprit.

"Today I came in early and found the phone at the reception ringing. It was Admissions office from Thouyandou University and they wanted confirmation that you were cancelling your application."

"What?"

"Yes, I was surprised too. I mean you have been doing everything to get your life back on the track and to make sure you are able to stand on your own. I promised you that I would pay your tuition but now you want to quit? What is the meaning of all this?" Theo asked with genuine concern on his face.

I didn't know how to answer, but what I knew was he meant well. Theo was like family to me. A year ago after I got married, my parents decided to retire and go back home to Mozambique. They left Theo as a stand-in father. I had known Theo since I was six that was when my family had moved from Mozambique. We rented a house next-door to Theo and his wife. Theo helped my parents in finding jobs and enrolling me at a nearby primary school. Fourteen years later he was still helping me make a life worth living.

"You know what Raina? Go visit them at their offices. I am giving you the morning off. "Theo gave me a hand of dismissal, it didn't go well with his forty-something-year old face.

I thanked him and flew out of his office. If I were to show my honestly and commitment, I had to sort out this mess and be back in the office within the hour or two. First I had to rush to an ATM, I was running low on cash.

****

I sat for almost an hour in Admissions office. The registrar had gone to lunch and wasn't expected to be back before 2 o'clock. I waited still.

"May I ask what it, this meeting with the registrar, regarding to?" The assistant asked when she finally took notice of me.

"I received a call this morning saying I was cancelling my registration. I am here to correct the mistake and verify my registration." I answered.

"Sure no problem, what is your name."

"Raina Mchigo." I continued, "What? Why are you looking at me like that?"

"Is this a joke?" The assistant looked irritated and I couldn't tell why. "Raina Mchigo was the last person the registrar talked to before she left for lunch. The real Raina was here, she confirmed her cancellation from the university."

I could feel blood draining from my face. Surely this was a joke or a mistake of great magnitude. I pulled out my ID card and tried to explain. The assistant wouldn't have any of it. She threatened to call security if I didn't leave. I walked away in shame.

I started walking towards the city center. I didn't have any cash on me. Earlier when I had tried to withdraw cash from the ATM my card had declined. I had been forced to use my last cash to board a taxi to the University. I started walking towards the nearest Capitec Bank offices I knew.

My phone rang; it was Suzie again. I declined the call. I wasn't in the right frame of mind to talk to her. Six months on and I haven't had the guts to block her calls off. Suzie called again.

"What Suzie?" I asked, "What do you want?"

"I know you have been texting my boyfriend, Raina." She claimed.

"No, I haven't."

"Don't lie I am looking at the messages. You asked for money and he transferred some into your bank account last night. I will let that one slide. But seriously girl you are begging my man to come back to you? What's wrong with you?" Suzie screams from the other end of the phone.

"I didn't ask him for money. He didn't send me any money. I haven't been begging him to crawl back. You have gone crazy you man stealing who..." she dropped the call before I could tell her what I actually thought of her.

It was better that way. If I had continued talking to her I would have cried and ruin my makeup. I wasn't about to make heads turn when I walked into the bank.

***

It was almost four pm when Theo finally arrived in front of the bank to pick me up. I had spent two hours sobbing. Few people had been polite enough to ask me what was wrong. I have lied and told them I was fine.

When Theo arrived, I scrambled up and made myself comfortable on the passenger seat. Then I moaned in agony. Just like any other father Theo tried to comfort me as his daughter. His request for me to explain what had happened fell on deaf ears.

During the wailing, the tear dropping and the mucus flowing I managed to tell him what had happened. I told him about my debit card dilemma and my decision to visit the bank with the issue.

"Then the bank teller told me that the account had been closed." I said to Theo.

"What about your money?" He asked in disbelief.

"She actually said a one named Raina Mchigo had withdrawn all the money before closing the account. The teller told me they were going to notify the police." I didn't feel any better telling my sad tale out loud.

Before he could say anything his cellphone rang. He continued listening for a while nodding his head.

110

"Yes she is here," Theo was glaring in my direction, "Honey please that's not true. Come on your know that's impossible. Listen to me darling..."

Theo started driving through the town. He had suddenly gone quiet. I started wondering if I had made a mistake to call him during my hour of need.

"That was my wife," Theo suddenly blurted out, "She told me you sent her a message saying you and I are having an affair."

"What?"

"Don't play dumb with me, Raina. I have been nothing but a Father figure to you and now you are saying I am your sugar daddy?" Theo's voice cracked in anger.

"No, that wasn't me I swear! Why would I do such a thing?" I tried to explain. I begged him to listen but he would not.

"Listen, Raina, I am tired of your games. Whatever this whole thing you are doing is not funny. You are fired and don't want to see you ever again. Now get out of my car!" He screamed at me as he hit the brakes. I jumped out of the car with questions on my mind and explanations on my lips.

******

Thouyandou is a scary place at night but it is quiet and peaceful enough to allow one to think straight. I sat on a bench near a service station. I couldn't explain the heck of the day I was having. For a certain, someone was impersonating me and ruining my life. Whatever her reasons were I didn't care, all I needed was my life back. And my money too.

I picked up my phone and called Theo's wife. She was still someone who would understand. I hoped she would understand.

"Thank you Raina for the tip. Just because you told me about the affair doesn't mean we are friends." Her greeting was icy cold.

"Listen Mama, I am not having an affair with your husband. I am not the one who sent you the message either. Just give me a minute to explain." I begged and fortunately she folded.

I told her everything from the first weird call from Suzie early that morning, to someone cancelling my registration at Thouyandou University. I told her about the imposter swindling money from my ex-husband and begging him to get back together. I didn't leave the part about the imposter withdrawing all my money from the bank and closing the account. I tried to explain to her it was that same person impersonating me that had sent the message about me having an affair with her husband.

"I have known you since you were six Raina, you are an honest person but that doesn't mean I believe you," she continued, "how are going to prove that it wasn't you but an imposter?"

"I don't know how and I don't think I can."

"Listen, about the imposter closing your bank account. That makes you the prime suspect in the embezzlement case at work. Theo told me you are trying to close the money trail and he has already gone to the police. I don't know if there is anything I can do." She hung up the phone.

It was at this moment I realised I was all alone. There was no one I could ask for advice or comfort. I could wait to be arrested and prove my innocence later but I didn't think it would work; no one would believe me. During these moments of doubt and pain Suzie had been the friend that gave me a shoulder to lean and cry on. For

14 years she had been my best friend. I decided to call her one last time. It went straight to voicemail.

"Hey Suzie it's me Raina. Listen I am in need of money to go back home to Mozambique. I am going to sell your laptop. I promise I will pay you back. Someone is impersonating me. She has stolen all my money and ruined my life. She is even committed a crime, now the police are after me. I will sneak out of the country and I will be back when I have figured this all out."

More books from the author

Solo collections

Dreams of paradise

Blue threads and other stories

Edited/ co-edited anthologies

The rules of the city

Prima anthology volume 1 (with Tafadzwa Chiwanza)

Zimbolicious anthology volume 8 (with Tendai R Mwanaka)

Mmap Fiction and Drama Series

If you have enjoyed *Blue threads and other stories,* consider these other fine books in **Mmap Fiction and Drama Series** from *Mwanaka Media and Publishing:*

The Water Cycle by Andrew Nyongesa
A Conversation…, A Contact by Tendai Rinos Mwanaka
A Dark Energy by Tendai Rinos Mwanaka
Keys in the River: New and Collected Stories by Tendai Rinos Mwanaka
How The Twins Grew Up/Makurire Akaita Mapatya by Milutin Djurickovic and Tendai Rinos Mwanaka
White Man Walking by John Eppel
The Big Noise and Other Noises by Christopher Kudyahakudadirwe
Tiny Human Protection Agency by Megan Landman
Ashes by Ken Weene and Umar O. Abdul
Notes From A Modern Chimurenga: Collected Struggle Stories by Tendai Rinos Mwanaka
Another Chance by Chinweike Ofodile
Pano Chalo/Frawn of the Great by Stephen Mpashi, translated by Austin Kaluba
Kumafulatsi by Wonder Guchu
The Policeman Also Dies and Other Plays by Solomon A. Awuzie
Fragmented Lives by Imali J Abala
In the Beyond by Talent Madhuku
Zororo Risina Zororo by Oscar Gwiriri
Sword of Vengeance by Olatubosun David
Finding A Way Home by Tendai Mwanaka

Your Epistle by Solomon A Awuzie
The Restless Run and Ruin of the Roaches and Rats by McLayode
The Reign of Terror by Ntando Gerald
Ibala Lyabwina Nama by Austin Kaluba
Daddy, Please Don't Kill Mama by Natisha Parsons
Pilate's Angels by Goodenough Mashego

Soon to be released

Conversation with my Mother by Wonder Guchu

https://facebook.com/MwanakaMediaAndPublishing/